Lectin Free Air Fryer Cookbook 2018

Simple & Tasty Lectin Free Recipes for Your Air Fryer (Reduce Inflammation, Lose Weight and Prevent Disease)

Jason Bove

Table of contents

INTRODUCTION

Lectin is a carbohydrate-binding protein that is found in plants and according to the popular book 'The Plant Paradox', it is the cause of inflammation and can increase the risk of cancer and obesity. In order to have a healthier lifestyle and better weight control, limiting lectin consumption is being promoted. This is a new word that is being thrown around a lot among nutritionists and followers of the current diet culture. There is a lot of misinformation regarding this topic and this book aims to demystify it and give clear guidance about how and why one should pursue it.

CHAPTER1: UNDERSTANDING THE LECTIN FREE DIET

What is the Lectin Free Diet?

According to some scientists, lectins are extremely harmful to the body. They are also linked to weight gain. This new diet aims to propose a plan in which one's lectin intake is limited by a list of foods to eat and not to eat. There are also supplements that one has to take during this diet. There are some foods that one has to avoid during this diet like squash, beans, peas, etc. and some are allowed. This book will inform you how this diet can help your body feel fresher by avoiding lectins found in different foods.

Who is Dr. Steven Gundry

'The Plant Paradox: The Hidden Dangers in "Healthy" Foods That Cause Disease and Weight Gain' is the New York Times bestselling book that greatly popularized the lectin-free diet. Its author, Dr. Steven R. Gundry, is a renowned cardiologist who now focuses on diet and supplement-based medicine. He revealed the dangers of lectin-containing foods that are popularly consumed in American culture. His book is a great resource for anyone who is looking for information on this diet.

Dr. Gundry completed his B.A. from Yale University in 1972 and earned a medical degree from Medical College of Georgia in 1977. He has done some groundbreaking research in infant heart transplant. He is now working on uncovering the hidden harmful effects of plant-based healthy diets.

What are the Lectins?

Lectins are found in almost all kinds of foods, but their concentration is high in the grains and legumes group. One cannot clearly state the amount of lectin in a certain food and one cannot be sure what type of lectin the food contains and whether it is actually harmful or not. They help in keeping molecules and cells together- basically, they have binding properties like helping red blood cells cluster, so they do have some important and beneficial functions such as keeping the immune system strong, fighting cancer and bacteria in the body. In plants, they are used to keep insects away and the nitrogen component aids plant growth. Here is something that makes this very binding property harmful for one's body-they stop the body from absorbing certain essential vitamins. This makes lectins antinutrients. Proteins enter the bloodstream through the intestine and if the lining of the intestine gets damaged by extra consumption of lectins, these proteins would not pass through it undigested. Poor protein digestion can cause various diseases. Intestinal putrefaction produces many dangerous carcinogenic gases, mercaptans, ammonia, amines, etc. Bad bacteria dominate in your colon when it is full of undigested protein and this can cause irritable bowel syndrome, constipation, and diarrhea. One may also experience abdominal pain, food allergies, leaky gut syndrome, headaches, heartburn, gallstones, etc.

The dangers of lectin can be clearly observed if one consumes undercooked plant foods, like kidney beans. The after effects have a great semblance of food poisoning symptoms like severe nausea, vomiting, and diarrhea. This is because it contains the lectin called phytohaemagglutinin. Slow cooking is hence not recommended for kidney bean preparation.

Benefits of Lectin Free Diet

1. A healthier digestive tract: Lectin-rich foods cause damage to the digestive tract as they disturb normal metabolism function. Lectin is not digestible, so it sticks to the membranes in the digestive tracts. This causes gastric distress. Adopting the lectin-free diet can help one achieve a cleaner digestive tract.

2. Cleanse your diet: As mentioned earlier, kidney beans, when not cooked well, can be very dangerous for your body. Most people suggest that soaking them in water helps in removing the lectin content but that is not enough. Foods like these are not included in the diet so you can avoid the dangerous effects of undercooked legumes and beans. Lab rats were given raw kidney beans in an experiment to observe the toxic effects of lectins and they experienced bacterial overgrowth and reduction in their intestinal wall lining. Hence it is recommended that one should not consume beans, peanuts, and soy in their raw form as the lectin content is very high and dangerous for the digestive system.

3. Ward off peptic ulcers: Peptic ulcers are injuries in the digestive tract of stomach or lower part of the esophagus. Lectin-free diet reduces the risk of developing ulcers.

4. Weight reduction: People with heart disease and other metabolic problems like high blood pressure, diabetes, excess cholesterol notices the considerable change by following this diet. The foods consumed during this diet help in reducing fat in the body. According to Dr. Gundry, lectins are known to 'stimulate weight gain' as they increase the synthesis of fat cells, according to studies done in vitro and cause leptin resistance. Leptin resistance is important to understand here since it is linked to

controlling your hunger. If there is a malfunction of leptin receptors, one would overeat and this would cause obesity.

5. Reverse auto-immune disease: According to a research by Dr. Gundry, 1200 patients with coronary heart disease followed this diet and did not need any surgery for their heart problems. Moreover, lectins are also known to increase the risk of heart disease, arthritis, dementia, and diabetes. The diet basically reduces the stickiness on the insides of blood vessels which eases the blood flow through them. This is highly beneficial for people with autoimmune disease, IBS, arthritis, migraines, brain fog, etc. The risk of autoimmune diseases increases because gut permeability is increased by consistent exposure of the gut to dietary lectins. Lectins are also mistaken to be pathogens inside the body due to their binding quality and are hence attacked by the body which starts an immune response in the body.

6. Lower inflammation: Lectin-free diet can reduce inflammation in the body.

CHAPTER2: AIR FRYER 101

What is an Air Fryer?

Cleaning up one's diet is important for cleaning the body but there is another component of the diet that we tend to ignore when we start a healthy lifestyle and that is- the cooking method. The way we cook the food we are going to consume plays a great role in its nutritious value and we must be careful about the appliances and products we use to cook. The Air fryer is the perfect answer for people who are trying to avoid frying and eat healthier food. Air fryer will give you the same effects of frying without the cholesterol-laden layer of oily food. Thanks to modern technology, we have now solved this predicament and people can avoid diseases like diabetes, hypertension, etc.

This appliance has gained a great deal of attention from health-savvy customers as it is an excellent substitute for traditional frying. One must be wondering how science managed to achieve this feat. This contraption uses only 20% oil and 80% air to circulate at very high speed. As this air passes over the food to be cooked, the food is done very quickly. There is a fan at the top of the compartment that blows air at high speed. What can be more amazing than having that 20% oil sucked out of the 'fried' food as well? There is a mechanism in the fryer that dries up the oil from the cooked food and you get nicely fried, healthy food that keeps your taste buds happy. One might wonder how this fryer can get the same products without following the conventional methods, but this has been made possible by the Maillard Effect which cooks food at 392 degrees Fahrenheit, so you get the same crispy, brown fried food.

Benefits of Air Fryer Cooking

There are some foods that do not require any oil addition in the fryer at all. These foods include frozen foodstuff to be baked, raw meat, fried chicken wings, roast chicken, steaks, pork chops, fish, French fries. You can add a tablespoon of oil for French fries, but it would still be delicious without the oil. All kinds of meat are cooked nice and well to the core as it circulates air at all angles. All one has to do is adjust the timer and temperature and let the food get cooked. In the end, you get a well cooked, healthy meal without the fat content. This is an amazing innovation for weight watchers and people trying to keep their cholesterol levels in check.

It is very easy to clean up the air fryer. There is a dish at the bottom that collects any fluids or crumbs from the food being cooked. The removable parts can be washed very easily, and they are made from a material that does not let things stick to it.

Apart from frying, air fryer has other functions as well- it can grill, roast and bake as well.

Another very notable benefit of the fryer is that is cooks in considerably lesser time as compared to traditional methods of frying. For people who are busy or always on the go, this is a good way to prepare meals at home. You can even cook more than one dish at a time due to the separators in the cooking compartment.

Keeping Your Device Clean

The basket must be cleaned as food gets stuck to it and if one doesn't wash it right after cooking, it can leave a bad smell in the fryer and kitchen. In order to clean the basket, take a container and fill it with liquid soap, baking soda can be used as well, and water. The basket should be left to soak in it for about 10 minutes. Using a sponge or brush, scrape off the dirt, no hard bristle brush. Wash the basket with water to clean off the soap and wash the pan in a similar fashion. Do not forget to clean the outside of the fryer as well, use moist cloth.

The coil only needs to be cleaned four times a year. When there is smoke coming out of the vent, it is a sign that the coil needs cleaning. Before cleaning the coil, allow the fryer to cool and unplug it. Then invert it and clean the coil with moist tissue and use a soft brush. Dry the coil with a towel.

Cooking Time of Various Foods

Food	Cooking Temperature(°F)	Cooking Time (minutes)
Vegetable		
Broccoli	400	6
Carrots	380	15
Cauliflower	400	12
Corn on the cob	390	6
Eggplant	400	15
Mushrooms	400	5
Onions	400	10
Potatoes	400	12
Tomatoes	350	10

Chicken		
Breast	380	12
Drumsticks	370	20
Thighs (bone in)	380	22
Legs (bone in)	380	30
Wings	400	12
Beef		
Burger	370	16-20
Meatballs	380	10
Flank steak	400	12
Pork and lamb		
Bacon	400	5-7
Sausages	380	15
Pork chop, bone in	400	12
Seafood		
Fish fillet	400	10
Salmon, fillet	380	12
Shrimp	400	5
Scallops	400	5-7
Frozen food		
French fries	400	18
Fish sticks	400	10
Chicken nuggets	400	10

Pros and Cons of the Air Fryer

Pros

When you have a craving for fried foods, but you still want to eat healthily, there is not in any healthy frying option out there that you can try. Air fryer can quickly serve you hot, crispy dishes like onion rings, chicken wings, chicken nuggets, fries, etc. without using a large amount of oil.

One advantage that makes air fryer better than an oven is that it is much more efficient regarding the electricity consumption. The cost of cooking is lesser because the cooking time is greatly reduced, and your house does not get heat up in the process which is a big nuisance in the summer.

Air fryers can be used for a huge variety of cooking methods- roasting, grilling, steaming, reheating that is better than microwave, baking, etc. As can be seen in the previous section, there is a very large variety of the kinds of foods you can cook in an air fryer due to the different kinds of functions it has.

People with small kitchen do not have to worry at all as this appliance is only the size of an average coffee maker. Once you get the hang of it, air fryer is very easy to convenient to use.

Cons

When buying the air fryer, make sure that the material it is made from is durable. Most of the time, it is not worth your money and the heating element, controls and fan stop working. The washable parts should also be hard and sturdy. Finding a good manufacturer can be hard.

It is not an ideal cooker for big families because it cannot cook in large quantities. It can serve 4 people at most.

Everyone who is new to the fryer will make mistakes in the beginning and it takes time to develop an understanding of the cooking time and temperature for different dishes. There is also a lot of the wrong estimation of the size of the meal that can be cooked in it and sometimes food would get stuck in the basket which makes cleaning up very hard. Some people find it difficult to adjust to this new way of cooking.

Top 3 Air Fryer as Your Choice

There is a wide range of brands in the market that can make you confused and indecisive about which one to choose for your need and budget. This section will try to address those qualms as it discusses the three most popular brands of air fryers in 2018.

The GoWISE 8 in 1 Air Fryer: It gives you the best value for your money. With the eight functions, it does a lot of work for one single fryer. The preprogrammed settings in the machine make it very easy for newbies to understand and cook without burning their food. It can cook a large quantity of food and has a power rating of 1500 watt compared to 2100 watts of the Philips Air Fryer. Users can also have a great deal of freedom with temperature change as you can choose from any temperature between 176 and 392 degrees. The only con of this fryer is that it can cook for 30 minutes in a single session.

Philips XL Air fryer: This must be the one that you have heard the most about online, but it is less cost-effective than the GoWISE brand. As mentioned before, the power rating might not be very affordable for many people. It can cook a large quantity at one time as well (serves four people). This is a heavy appliance, but it has more functions than the GoWISE one, so you can get this one if you are ready to make a big investment.

T-Fal Actifry: This model is a little more expensive than the GoWISE but it has more qualities than that one. It is manufactured better, and the basket is sturdier than the GoWISE machine. The warranty of the basket included shows that the company has made it very durable. The quantity of food that can be cooked is average and it cannot cook for more than 4 people. This is a dishwasher friendly appliance so cleaning it up is much easier. GoWISE can only cook for 30 minutes at once while Actifry does it for 99 minutes straight which is a commendable feat for a lightweight machine. It has no temperature control so one would not have to worry about that setting but this could be a problem for some people. The cookbook that comes along it can help people figure out what to do about the time settings for different foods.

You can make the wisest and smartest decision based on these three top choices in the market.

CHAPTER3: FOOD TO EAT AND FOOD TO AVOID

A lectin-intolerant individual should focus on eating organic food and make sure they are peeled and have no seed as most of the pectin is present in a peel or seeds of fruit or vegetables. The following foods are said to have lower lectin content, so they are recommended by Dr. Gundry to include in your lectin free diet:

- Mushrooms
- Avocado
- Garlic
- Onion
- Peppers, seeded
- Tomato, peeled and seeded
- Zucchinis, peeled and seeded
- Asparagus
- Celery
- Olives
- Pure avocado oil
- Extra virgin oil
- Pasture-raised meats
- Leafy green vegetables
- A2 milk, unsweetened
- Apple cider vinegar, with mother
- Broccoli
- Brussels sprouts
- Sweet potatoes
- Butter from almonds or nuts
- Walnuts
- Pistachios
- Pecans
- Pine nuts
- White sesame seeds
- Miso
- Chili flakes
- Fish, wild caught

- Eggs
- Beef
- Bok choy
- Cauliflower
- Pumpkin
- Squash
- Carrot
- Berries
- Citrus fruits
- Pineapple
- Cherries
- Apples
- Sugar-free and homemade sauces

Foods that you should avoid during your lectin free diet are as follows. This may feel like a lot of nutrient-rich foods are eliminated from your diet and the sources of fiber are almost nonexistent, so one has to take supplements to regulate bowel movements.

- Peas
- Peanuts
- Lentils
- Squash
- Potatoes
- Eggplant
- Fruits that are not in-season
- Grains
- Corn
- Meat from corn-fed animals
- A1 milk
- Soybeans
- Kidney beans
- Pinto beans
- Navy beans
- Lima beans

- Fava beans
- Wax beans
- Castor beans
- String beans
- Mung beans
- Field beans
- Black beans
- Lentils
- Wheat
- Rye
- Malt
- Oat
- Barley
- Rice
- Sunflower seeds
- Black Sesame Seeds
- Almonds
- Hazelnuts
- Cashews
- Goji berries
- Beets
- Cucumbers
- Rhubarb
- Turnips
- Watermelon
- Yogurt
- Cheese
- Chocolate

CHAPTER4: TIPS AND FQAS

What is the function of lectins in plants?

Lectins are a kind of defense mechanism for plants that helps them fight organisms that try to eat them. The sticky lectins are used to make the insects paralyzed.

If lectins are useful for plants, why are they toxic to humans?

They bind to the walls of the intestines by sticking to the sugars on the walls of the intestine. Not only are these sugars found on the inside of the intestine but also in the mouth, nose, and saliva. In the gut, lectins are known to create gaps in the intestinal cells which then cause several dangerous bacteria and lipopolysaccharides to enter the bloodstream and wreak havoc.

Vegetables and beans are supposed to be healthy. Why are they toxic?

They are healthy, but they can be very dangerous for people who are sensitive to lectins or have risks of developing the diseases that over-consumption of lectins can stimulate.

What is the leaky gut?

This word has been associated with the dangers for a long time, so it is good to inform yourself on the subject. Leaky gut, as its name suggests, is a lesion in the intestinal wall caused by lectins a lot of waste can get through it- partially digested food, bacteria, viruses, toxins, etc. When one's body picks up the presence of this trash, it sends emergency alarms throughout the body that then initiate the first aid response which is inflammation.

The leaky gut syndrome is a very painful condition in which the patient suffers from constipation, regular diarrhea, flatulence and bloating. If one keeps eating lectin-rich diet regularly, then the inflammation gets chronic and these gut problems get more frequent. This leads to autoimmune diseases as your body senses danger from inside all the time.

Can lectins also cause heart disease?

Heart disease is mainly caused by dysfunction in the blood vessels. Lectins are a major cause of this dysfunction as they are responsible for making the immune system attack the blood vessels. To prove the correlation between blood vessel dysfunction and lectins, Dr. Gundry put 200 patients, with the risk of developing heart disease, in an experiment where he fed them on a low lectin diet with supplements. The lectin-free diet contained olive oil, grass-fed beef, leafy greens, and fish. The supplements had several vitamins and polyphenols from fish. By following this plan for six months, more than half of the patients had reversed the damage on their blood vessels.

Is Quinoa lectin free?

Quinoa is a safe gluten-free product but there is no guarantee about it being lectin-free as the lectin-high grains get mixed in the quinoa components where the grains are processed. Due to this contamination, it is hard to say that quinoa is safe for a lectin free diet.

Do bananas have lectins?

Yes, bananas contain proteins called Musa acuminate L which is now identified as a lectin. Bananas will not be safe to consume in a lectin-free diet.

Does fermentation reduce lectins?

Fermenting and sprouting can help in reducing the lectin content of some foods. This happens because the friendly bacteria process the anti-nutrients and lectins are reduced by 95%.

Does soaking nuts remove lectins?

Yes, soaking and sprouting both help in somewhat removing the lectins from grains, legumes, nuts, and seeds. This only removes 50% of them.

What are lectin blockers?

It is a unique blend of powerful compounds that are designed to stick to the lectins in your diet. This helps in regulating bowel movements.

How do lectin blockers work?

They are made of deflects, which is basically blocking sugars. They are sacrificial molecules that attach to the carbohydrate receptors on lectins and this makes them incapable of sticking to the cells in the body.

Do lectins also cause brain disease?

The FASEB Journal and the American Gastrointestinal Association has proven that Parkinson's disease is caused when lectins move up the vagus nerve to the brain. Moreover, Alzheimer's disease is also caused by a leaky gut which is a harmful effect of lectins.

How can vegetarians follow the lectin-free diet?

A vegetarian diet is heavy in lectin content but there are ways to eat vegetables that can help ease the body of the lectin after effects. You can try different methods like peeling nightshade vegetables and removing their seeds, soaking beans overnight in baking soda, pressure cooking beans, fermenting fruits and vegetables. One such example is kimchi.

TIPS

1. Corn fed meat is not allowed on the diet and that means lectin-free diet followers cannot get meat from grocery stores. Try to get meat that is grass fed and endorsed by American Grassfed Association

2. A1 milk is not good for your health as it causes an autoimmune reaction in your gut. A2 milk can be easily available where farmers have grass-fed cows.

3. Soy can be consumed if it is traditionally fermented.

4. There are some beans that you can consume from time to time on your lectin free diet. These include rice beans, cowpeas, broad beans, lupin seeds, Polish peas and raw green beans as they have low to moderate lectin content.

5. Before cooking beans, soak them in water for at least 12 hours. Keep changing the water. A very helpful tip is to add baking soda to the water in which it is soaked. This neutralizes beans even further. Then when you are cooking the beans, cook them on high heat initially. Cooking them in a pressure cooker is the best way to go.

6. When consuming potatoes, roasting or steaming is a good option to remove resistant starch.

7. There are some safe lectins that should be mentioned here: cooked tubers (sweet potatoes, yucca, and taro) and authentic extra-virgin olive oil.

8. When eating fruits and vegetables, remove the skin, hull, and seeds as these contain the highest amount of lectin. De-skinned almonds are a good option for people on lectin free diet.

9. Choose white over brown. White bread and rice are better than brown substitutes for following the lectin free diet. Raising the bread by yeast or sourdough breaks down gluten and harmful glutens so it is safer to consume it that way.

10. A pressure cooker is a very helpful appliance to have around the kitchen if you are trying to remove lectins from your food. The slow cooker is not a good option because it increases lectin content.

11. Peanuts are a very good source of healthy nutrients like protein, unsaturated fats, minerals, and vitamins. They contain lectins, but they are not a danger to health otherwise.

12. Seaweeds and mucilaginous vegetables are good lectin blockers as they bind to the lectins and do not allow them to stick to the cells in the body.

13. Lectins are not affected by dry heat so raw legume flours or its products should be avoided.

14. Read labels and keep a food journal in order to track what you eat and avoid lectins more effectively.

15. According to the severity of your allergies or body's sensitivities, you should decide how much you want to limit lectin content in your diet. Find foods that are relatively safer for your body type. People with autoimmune disorders are more susceptible to the harmful effects of lectin. Through experimenting and observing your body's reaction to the lectin high foods that you consume, you can see which ones affect you badly and how you can reduce their consumption.

CHAPTER 5: BREAKFAST RECIPES
Pancakes with Tigernut Flour and Wild Blueberries

| Servings: 4 pancakes |
| Preparation time: 10 minutes | Cooking time: 6 minutes | Total time: 16 minutes |

Ingredients:

- 1/4 cup wild blueberries, frozen
- 1/2 cup and 1 tablespoon Tigernut flour
- 1/8 teaspoon salt
- 3 teaspoons green banana powder
- 1 teaspoon vanilla extract, unsweetened
- 1 egg, pasture raised
- 1/2 cup coconut milk, unsweetened
- Coconut butter for serving

Method:
- Crack an egg in a bowl, whisk in milk until combined and then stir in flour until incorporated.
- Mix in salt, banana powder, and vanilla and then fold in berries until just mix.
- Switch on a 6-quarts air fryer, set temperature to 100 degrees C or 220 degrees F and time to 5 minutes to preheat it.
- Grease an air fryer proof pan with a cooking spray and spread prepared batter into it in four portions.
- Insert pan into the air fryer, set frying time to 3 minutes and let fry.
- Then check pancakes by pulling out the pan and if the bottom has turned golden brown, then turn pancakes using tongs.
- Insert pan back into the fryer and let fry for another 3 minutes or until pancakes are cooked through.
- When fryer beeps, transfer pancakes to a platter using tongs and serve with butter.

Cinnamon Cassava Flour Pancakes

| Servings: 4 |
| Preparation time: 10 minutes | Cooking time: 14 minutes | Total time: 24 minutes |

Ingredients:

- 1 cup cassava flour
- 1 tablespoon baking powder
- 1/4 teaspoon sea salt
- 2 tablespoons erythritol sweetener
- 1 teaspoon ground cinnamon and more for serving
- 1/8 teaspoon ground nutmeg
- 1/2 teaspoon vanilla extract, unsweetened
- 3 tablespoons melted coconut butter and more for serving
- 2 eggs, pasture raised
- 1 1/4 cup almond yogurt
- 1/4 cup water

Method:

- Place flour in a bowl and stir in baking powder, salt, erythritol, cinnamon, and nutmeg until mixed.
- Crack eggs in another bowl and whisk in vanilla, yogurt, and water until well combined.
- Whisk in flour mixture, 2 tablespoons at a time, until incorporated and smooth.
- Switch on a 6-quarts air fryer, set temperature to 199 degrees C or 390 degrees F and time to 5 minutes to preheat it.
- Grease an air fryer proof pan with a non-stick cooking spray and spread prepared batter into it with some distance between pancakes, don't overcrowd the pan.
- Insert pan into the air fryer, set frying time to 4 minutes and let fry.
- Then check pancakes by pulling out the pan and if the bottom has turned golden brown, then turn pancakes using tongs.
- Insert pan back into the fryer and let fry for another 3 minutes or until pancakes are cooked through.

- When fryer beeps, transfer pancakes to a platter using tongs and use remaining batter to cook more pancakes.
- Serve with coconut butter.

Sweet Potato Hash

| Servings: 4 |
| Preparation time: 10 minutes | Cooking time: 15 minutes | Total time: 25 minutes |

Ingredients:

- 2 medium-sized sweet potatoes, peeled and small diced
- ½ teaspoon onion powder
- 1 tablespoon minced garlic
- ½ teaspoon sea salt
- 1/2 teaspoon ground black pepper
- 1 teaspoon smoked paprika
- ½ teaspoon turmeric powder
- 2 tablespoons avocado oil, pure
- Scallions, green parts only sliced

Method:

- Grease an air fryer baking pan, add sweet potatoes and season with onion powder, salt, black pepper, paprika, and turmeric.
- Switch on a 6-quarts air fryer, set temperature to 180 degrees C or 350 degrees F and time to 5 minutes to preheat it.
- Insert pan into the air fryer, set frying time to 15 minutes and let cook until cooked through.
- When cooked halfway, pull out fryer pan, shake sweet potatoes using a wooden spoon and insert pan back into the fryer until cooking time is over.
- In the last five minutes, add garlic to hash browns and let cook until fragrant.
- When fryer beeps, transfer hash brown to a serving platter, top with scallions and serve with scrambled eggs.

Jicama Hash Browns

| Servings: 8 hash browns |
| Preparation time: 30 minutes | Cooking time: 15 minutes | Total time: 45 minutes |

Ingredients:

- 1 medium Jicama, peeled and grated
- ½ of a medium yellow onion, peeled and chopped
- 1 tablespoon minced garlic
- 2 eggs, pasture raised

Method:
- Press grated jicama in a sieve to drain excess water and add to a bowl.
- Crack eggs in it, then add onion and garlic and whisk until combined.
- Spread this mixture in a plate, pat firmly and let freeze for 20 minutes.
- After 20 minutes, switch on a 6-quarts air fryer, set the temperature to 180 degrees C or 350 degrees F and time to 5 minutes to preheat it.
- When ready to fry, use a knife to divide hash browns into equal pieces and add to a greased air fryer basket.
- Insert pan into the air fryer, set frying time to 15 minutes and let fry until crispy and nicely browned.
- When cooked halfway, pull out fryer basket, shake chicken using tongs and insert basket back into the fryer until cooking time is over.
- When fryer beeps, transfer hash browns to a serving plate and serve with ketchup.

Bagels

| Servings: 8 bagels |
me: 25 minutes | Cooking time: 18 minutes | Total time: 35 minutes |

- 3 cups almond flour, blanched
- 2 teaspoons baking powder
- 2 teaspoons sea salt
- 2 tablespoons coconut sugar
- 1 cup tapioca starch
- 2 tablespoons apple cider vinegar, organic
- 1 egg yolk, slightly beaten
- 2/3 cup water, warmed
- Poppy seeds as needed for topping

Method:

- Place flour in a bowl and stir in baking powder, salt, and starch until mixed.
- Whisk in honey, vinegar, and water until smooth dough comes together.
- Divide this dough into 8 portions and roll each portion into balls with hands dusted with starch.
- Working on one ball at a time, flatten it and push one finger through the center of the ball to make a bagel shape.
- Prepare remaining bagels in the same manner.
- Place a large pot half full of water over high heat, and when comes to boil, stir in salt.
- Add bagels to boiling water, 3 to 4 bagels at a time, let cook for 1 minute and then remove them using a slotted spoon.
- Switch on a 6-quarts air fryer, set temperature to 165 degrees C or 330 degrees F and time to 5 minutes to preheat it.
- Place bagels into a greased fryer basket, don't overcrowd the basket, then brush bagels with egg yolk and top with poppy seeds.

- Insert fryer basket into the air fryer, set frying time to 10 minutes and let cook until top is nicely browned.
- When cooked halfway, pull out fryer basket, shake bagels using tongs and insert basket back into the fryer until cooking time is over.
- Cook remaining bagels in the same manner and serve.

Sweet Potato Toasts with Guacamole

| Servings: 6 toasts |
| Preparation time: 10 minutes | Cooking time: 20 minutes | Total time: 22 minutes |

Ingredients:

- 1 large sweet potato, organic
- 2 medium avocados, organic
- 1 tablespoon chopped organic cilantro, organic
- 1 organic jalapeno, seeded and diced
- 1 tablespoon diced yellow onion, organic
- 1 tablespoon minced garlic, organic
- 1/4 teaspoon sea salt
- 1/8 teaspoon black ground pepper, organic
- 1 teaspoon lime juice, organic and fresh
- Boiled eggs, pasture raised for serving

Method:
- Cut each end of the sweet potato and then cut horizontally into 4 to 6 slices, each ¼ inch slices.
- Switch on a 6-quarts air fryer, set temperature to 149 degrees C or 300 degrees F and time to 5 minutes to preheat it.
- Grease air fryer basket with oil, and brush sweet potato slices with oil and add to air fryer basket.
- Insert fryer basket into the air fryer, set frying time to 20 minutes and let cook until crispy and nicely browned.
- When cooked halfway, pull out fryer basket, turn sweet potato slices using tongs and insert basket back into the fryer until cooking time is over.
- In the meantime, prepare guacamole.
- For this, peel and core avocados and place its flesh in a bowl.
- Add remaining ingredients and mash using a fork until smooth and set aside until required.

- When fryer beeps, transfer sweet potato slices to plate and cook remaining sweet potato in the same manner.
- Top slices of sweet potatoes with guacamole and serve with sliced eggs and avocado.

Frittata

| Servings: 1 Frittata |

| Preparation time: 10 minutes | Cooking time: 17 minutes | Total time: 27 minutes |

Ingredients:

- 1/2 cup broccoli florets, organic
- 1/2 cup organic red bell pepper, seeded and sliced
- ½ teaspoon salt
- ½ teaspoon ground black pepper
- 3 eggs, pasture raised
- 2 tbsp coconut milk
- 2 tbsp grated cheddar cheese, organic and lactose-free

Method:

- Switch on a 6-quarts air fryer, set temperature to 180 degrees C or 350 degrees F and time to 5 minutes to preheat it.
- In the meantime, grease an air-fryer baking sheet and add broccoli florets and peppers.
- Insert pan into the air fryer, set frying time to 7 minutes and let cook.
- In the meantime, whisk together eggs, salt, black pepper and coconut milk until smooth.
- When fryer beeps, remove the pan, evenly pour egg mixture over vegetables and sprinkle cheese over top.
- Return pan into the air fryer and cook for 10 minutes or until frittata is cooked through.
- Serve when ready.

Spanakopita Omelet

| Servings: 1 |
| Preparation time: 5 minutes | Cooking time: 20 minutes | Total time: 30 minutes |

Ingredients:

- 2 cups organic spinach, chopped
- 1/4 cup minced yellow onion, organic
- 1 cup organic parsley, chopped
- ½ teaspoon minced garlic
- ½ teaspoon salt
- ½ teaspoon ground black pepper
- 1 tablespoon crumbled feta cheese, lactose-free
- 1/2 teaspoon dried oregano
- 1/2 teaspoon dried thyme
- 2 eggs

Method:
- Switch on a 6-quarts air fryer, set temperature to 180 degrees C or 350 degrees F and time to 5 minutes to preheat it.
- In the meantime, crack eggs in a bowl and season with salt and black pepper.
- Add spinach, onion, and parsley and whisk until mixed.
- Take an air fryer proof pan, grease with oil and add omelet batter in it.
- Insert pan into the air fryer, set frying time to 10 minutes and let cook until top is nicely golden brown, and omelet is cooked through.
- When cooked halfway, pull out fryer basket and sprinkle oregano and thyme on top of omelet along with cheese.
- When fryer beeps, remove the pan from air fryer, lose its sides and transfer to plate.
- Garnish with parsley and serve.

33

Olive Oil Sesame Cookies

| Servings: 14 cookies |
| Preparation time: 15 minutes | Cooking time: 15 minutes | Total time: 30 minutes |

Ingredients:

- 1 cup almond flour, blanched
- 3/4 cup green banana flour
- 3/4 teaspoon baking soda
- 1/4 cup white sesame seeds
- 1/8 teaspoon salt
- 2 tablespoons erythritol sweetener
- 1 scoop Turmeric Tonic
- 1 organic lemon, zested
- 4 tablespoons lemon juice, organic and fresh
- 1/2 cup olive oil

Method:
- Place flours in a bowl and stir in baking soda, sesame seeds, salt and turmeric tonic until mixed.
- Beat together sweetener, lemon zest, and oil until incorporated and then beat in lemon juice until well combined.
- Stir in flour mixture, 2 tablespoons at a time, until incorporated and smooth dough comes together, don't over mix.
- Switch on a 6-quarts air fryer, set temperature to 180 degrees C or 350 degrees F and time to 5 minutes to preheat it.
- Divide dough into 14 portions, then roll them into balls and slightly flatten them.
- Line fryer basket with aluminum foil, then place cookies on foil, don't overcrowd the pan and insert basket into the air fryer.
- Set frying time to 15 minutes and let cook until top nicely browned.
- When fryer beeps, transfer cookies to a plate and cook remaining if any cookies are left.
- Let cookies cool slightly before serving.

Falafel

| Servings: 5 |

| Preparation time: 1 hour and 40 minutes | Cooking time: 24 minutes | Total time: 2 hours and 4 minutes |

Ingredients:

- 4 tablespoons almond flour and more for coating
- 2 medium organic sunchokes, peeled and boiled
- 1 small head of cauliflower, steamed
- 2 medium organic parsnips, peeled and boiled
- 1/2 cup organic parsley, fresh
- 1 organic leek, diced
- 4 cloves of garlic, peeled
- 1 1/2 teaspoon salt
- 1/4 teaspoon ground black pepper
- 1/4 teaspoon cayenne pepper
- 2 teaspoons ground cumin
- 1 teaspoon ground coriander
- 1/8 teaspoon ground cardamom
- White sesame seeds as needed for coating
- 2 tablespoons ground turmeric

Method:
- Place all ingredients except for sesame seeds and turmeric in a food processor and pulse until mashed but not quite.
- Tip the mixture in a bowl, cover with a lid and let refrigerate for 1 hour and 30 minutes.
- When ready to cook, switch on a 6-quarts air fryer, set temperature to 190 degrees C or 370 degrees F and time to 5 minutes to preheat it.
- Shape 1/3rd of the mixture into falafels and coat with almond flour.
- Shape 1/3rd of remaining mixture into falafels and coat with sesame seeds.
- Stir in turmeric into remaining mixture and shape into falafels.

- Grease air fryer basket with oil, brush falafels with oil and add to basket, don't overcrowd basket and keep remaining falafels in the refrigerator until required for frying.
- Insert fryer basket into the air fryer, set frying time to 12 minutes and let fry until nicely browned.
- When cooked halfway, pull out fryer basket, turn falafels using tongs and insert basket back into the fryer until cooking time is over.
- When fryer beeps, transfer falafels to plate and fry remaining falafels in the same manner.
- Serve with hummus.

CHAPTER 6: APPETIZER & SNACK RECIPES
Cauliflower Bites

| Servings: 1 |
| Preparation time: 5 minutes | Cooking time: 6 minutes | Total time: 11 minutes |

Ingredients:

- 1 1/2 cups florets of organic cauliflower
- 1 teaspoon sea salt
- ¾ teaspoon ground black pepper, organic
- 1 tablespoon avocado oil, pure

Method:
- Switch on a 6-quarts air fryer, set temperature to 199 degrees C or 390 degrees F and time to 5 minutes to preheat it.
- In the meantime, cut cauliflower into ½-inch slices, then add to bowl and season with salt, black pepper, and oil.
- Place seasoned cauliflower slices in a greased air fryer basket and insert into the air fryer.
- Set frying time to 6 minutes and let cook until crispy and nicely browned.
- When cooked halfway, pull out fryer basket, shake cauliflower slices using tongs and insert basket back into the fryer until cooking time is over.
- When fryer beeps, transfer cauliflower slices to a plate and serve.

Fried Artichokes

| Servings: 4 |
| Preparation time: 10 minutes | Cooking time: 8 minutes | Total time: 18 minutes |

Ingredients:

- 1/2 cup almond flour
- 14-ounce artichoke hearts, organic
- 1/2 teaspoon ground garlic, organic
- 1/2 teaspoon salt
- 1/2 teaspoon ground cayenne pepper, organic
- 1/2 cup nutritional yeast
- 1 tablespoon avocado oil, pure

Method:

- Drain artichoke hearts, then cut each into the half, slice thinly and place in a bowl.
- Add oil and toss until coated.
- Stir together remaining ingredients in a separate bowl until mixed well and then sprinkle on artichoke hearts.
- Toss to coat and then transfer artichoke hearts into an air fryer basket.
- Switch on a 6-quarts air fryer, set temperature to 182 degrees C or 360 degrees F and time to 5 minutes to preheat it.
- Then insert fryer basket into the air fryer, set frying time to 8 minutes and let cook until crispy and nicely browned.
- When cooked halfway, pull out fryer basket, turn artichoke hearts using tongs and insert basket back into the fryer until cooking time is over.
- When fryer beeps, transfer artichoke hearts to a plate and serve with guacamole.

Avocado Egg Boats

| Servings: 2 |
| Preparation time: 5 minutes | Cooking time: 12 minutes | Total time: 17 minutes |

Ingredients:

- 1 large organic avocado, cored and halved
- 1 tablespoon fresh parsley, organic
- ½ teaspoon salt
- ½ teaspoon ground black pepper
- 2 eggs

Method:
- Switch on a 6-quarts air fryer, set temperature to 205 degrees C or 400 degrees F and time to 5 minutes to preheat it.
- In the meantime, cut avocado into half and remove its core.
- Place avocado halves into greased air fryer basket and insert it into the air fryer.
- Set frying time to 12 minutes and let fry until egg is cooked to desired doneness.
- When fryer beeps, transfer avocados to a serving plate, garnish with parsley and serve.

Avocado Fries

| Servings: 1 |
| Preparation time: 15 minutes | Cooking time: 10 minutes | Total time: 25 minutes |

Ingredients:

- 1 large avocado, organic
- 3 tablespoons arrowroot powder, organic
- ½ teaspoon onion powder, organic
- 1 teaspoon garlic powder, organic
- ¼ teaspoon salt
- ½ teaspoon ground black pepper, organic
- ½ teaspoon smoked paprika, organic
- ¾ cup shredded coconut, unsweetened
- 1 egg, pasture raised

Method:
- Cut avocado into half, remove its core and then slice each half into 5 pieces.
- Place arrowroot powder in a bowl and stir in ¼ teaspoon onion powder, ½ teaspoon garlic powder, 1/8 teaspoon salt, ¼ teaspoon each of black pepper and paprika.
- Place coconut in another bowl, add remaining seasoning and stir until mixed.
- Crack an egg in a bowl and whisk slightly.
- Working on one avocado slice at a time, cover slice with arrowroot mixture, then dip slice into egg and coat with coconut mixture.
- Coat remaining avocado slices in the same manner, then place in a greased air fryer basket and coat onions with non-stick cooking.
- Switch on a 6-quarts air fryer, set temperature to 199 degrees C or 390 degrees F and time to 10 minutes to preheat it.
- When cooked halfway, pull out fryer basket, shake avocado fries using tongs and insert basket back into the fryer until cooking time is over.
- When fryer beeps, transfer to a serving plate and serve with favorite dip.

Onion Rings

| Servings: 4 |
| Preparation time: 15 minutes | Cooking time: 10 minutes | Total time: 25 minutes |

Ingredients:

- 10-ounce organic yellow onions
- 1/2 cup almond flour, blanched
- 1/4 teaspoon onion powder, organic
- 1/2 teaspoon garlic powder, organic
- 1/2 teaspoon salt
- 1/4 teaspoon ground black pepper, organic
- 1 ¼ teaspoon smoked paprika, organic
- 1 cup almond meal, organic
- 1 egg, pasture raised
- 1 tablespoon water

Method:

- Peel onion, then slice into 1/2-inch thick round pieces and separate each round into 6 to 7 rings.
- Place flour in a bowl, add 1 teaspoon paprika and stir in ¼ teaspoon salt until mixed.
- Crack an egg in another bowl, add water and whisk slightly.
- Place almond meal in another bowl, add remaining ingredients and stir until mixed.
- Cover onion with flour mixture, then dip into egg and cover with almond meal mixture until coat completely.
- Coat remaining onion rings in the same manner, then place into a greased air fryer basket in a single layer and coat onions with non-stick cooking.
- Switch on a 6-quarts air fryer, set temperature to 191 degrees C or 375 degrees F and time to 5 minutes to preheat it.
- Insert fryer basket into the air fryer, set frying time to 10 minutes and let cook until crispy and nicely browned.

- When cooked halfway, pull out fryer basket, turn onion rings using tongs and insert basket back into the fryer until cooking time is over.
- When fryer beeps, transfer onion rings to a serving plate and cook remaining onion rings in the same manner.
- Serve onion rings with favorite dip.

Chipotle Broccoli Fritters

| Servings: 6 fritters |
| Preparation time: 10 minutes | Cooking time: 8 minutes | Total time: 18 minutes |

Ingredients:

- 1 3/4 cup almond meal, organic
- 2 cups shredded broccoli florets
- 1/2 of a medium yellow onion, chopped
- 1 teaspoon minced garlic, organic
- 1 tablespoon garlic powder, organic
- 1 teaspoon salt, organic
- ¾ teaspoon ground black pepper, organic
- 2 eggs, pasture raised

Method:
- Place all the ingredients in a large bowl, stir until well combined and shape mixture into 5 to 6 fritter balls.
- Switch on a 6-quarts air fryer, set temperature to 180 degrees C or 356 degrees F and time to 5 minutes to preheat it.
- Cover air fryer basket with parchment sheet, place fritter balls in it and then coat with non-sticking cooking spray.
- Insert fryer basket into the air fryer, set frying time to 8 minutes and let cook until crispy and nicely browned.
- When cooked halfway, pull out fryer basket, turn fritters using tongs and insert basket back into the fryer until cooking time is over.
- When fryer beeps, transfer fritters to serving platter using tongs and serve.

Sweet Potato Fries

| Servings: 1 |
| Preparation time: 10 minutes | Cooking time: 24 minutes | Total time: 34 minutes |

Ingredients:

- 12-ounce sweet potato, organic
- 1/2 teaspoon salt
- 1/2 teaspoon ground black pepper, organic
- 1/2 teaspoon cayenne pepper, organic
- 1/2 teaspoon turmeric powder, organic
- 2 tablespoons nutritional yeast
- 1 tablespoon avocado oil, pure

Method:

- Cut ends of sweet potato, then peel it and cut into ¼-inch thick French fries and place in a large bowl.
- Add oil and toss to coat.
- Add remaining ingredients, toss to coat and place into a greased air fryer basket in a single layer.
- Switch on a 6-quarts air fryer, set temperature to 205 degrees C or 400 degrees F and time to 5 minutes to preheat it.
- Insert fryer basket into the air fryer, set frying time to 8 minutes and let cook until crispy and nicely browned.
- When cooked halfway, pull out fryer basket, turn French fries using tongs and insert basket back into the fryer until cooking time is over.
- When fryer beeps, transfer French fries to a plate, cook remaining fries in the same manner and serve with favorite sauce.

Kale Crisps

| Servings: 4 |

| Preparation time: 5 minutes | Cooking time: 10 minutes | Total time: 15 minutes |

Ingredients:

- 1 bunch of organic kale, stems and ribs removed
- 1/2 teaspoon salt
- 1/4 teaspoon ground pepper
- 2 tablespoons avocado oil, pure

Method:

- Switch on a 6-quarts air fryer, set temperature to 199 degrees C or 390 degrees F and time to 5 minutes to preheat it.
- In the meantime, cut kale into 2-inch pieces and place in a bowl.
- Add salt, black pepper and oil, toss to coat and then place into fryer basket in a single layer.
- Insert fryer basket into the air fryer, set frying time to 5 minutes and let cook until crispy and nicely browned.
- When cooked halfway, pull out fryer basket, shake kale using tongs and insert basket back into the fryer until cooking time is over.
- Fry remaining kale in the same manner and serve.

CHAPTER 7: VEGETABLE RECIPES

Savory Roasted Asparagus

| Servings: 2 |
| Preparation time: 10 minutes | Cooking time: 10 minutes | Total time: 20 minutes |

Ingredients:

- ½ bunch of asparagus, organic
- ½ teaspoon garlic powder, organic
- ½ teaspoon salt
- ½ teaspoon ground black pepper, organic
- 1 organic lemon, juice

Method:

- Cut off the 2-inch bottom of asparagus and add to a bowl, add remaining ingredients and toss to coat.
- Switch on a 6-quarts air fryer, set temperature to 205 degrees C or 400 degrees F and time to 5 minutes to preheat it.
- In the meantime, place asparagus in a greased air fryer basket and then spray oil on asparagus.
- Insert fryer basket into the air fryer, set frying time to 10 minutes and let cook until cooked through and tender.
- When cooked halfway, pull out fryer basket, shake asparagus using tongs and insert basket back into the fryer until cooking time is over.
- Serve when ready.

Fried Okra

| Servings: 2 |

| Preparation time: 15 minutes | Cooking time: 10 minutes | Total time: 25 minutes |

Ingredients:

- 20 pods of okra, fresh
- 2/3 cup almond meal
- ½ teaspoon salt
- ½ teaspoon ground black pepper
- ½ teaspoon dried thyme
- ½ teaspoon garlic powder
- 2 eggs

Method:
- Crack eggs in a bowl and whisk.
- Cut okra into slices, add to eggs and toss to coat completely.
- Place remaining ingredients, except for salt, in another bowl, stir until mixed, then add okra and toss to coat.
- Switch on a 6-quarts air fryer, set temperature to 205 degrees C or 400 degrees F and time to 5 minutes to preheat it.
- Place okra into a greased air fryer basket, sprinkle with salt and then spray with oil.
- Insert fryer basket into the air fryer, set frying time to 10 minutes and let cook until crispy and nicely browned.
- When cooked halfway, pull out fryer basket, shake okra using tongs and insert basket back into the fryer until cooking time is over.
- Serve when done.

Garlic Mushrooms

| Servings: 12 |
| Preparation time: 15 minutes | Cooking time: 10 minutes | Total time: 25 minutes |

Ingredients:

- 12 chestnut mushrooms, organic
- ½ cup almond meal
- 1 teaspoon garlic powder
- ¾ teaspoon salt
- ½ teaspoon ground black pepper
- 1 tablespoon chopped parsley
- ¼ cup avocado oil, pure

Method:
- Stir together almond meal, garlic, salt, black pepper, and parsley until mixed and then stir in oil.
- Remove stalks of mushrooms and fill mushroom caps with almond meal mixture.
- Switch on a 6-quarts air fryer, set temperature to 200 degrees C or 392 degrees F and time to 5 minutes to preheat it.
- Place stuffed mushrooms in a single layer into a greased air fryer basket and insert it into the air fryer.
- Set frying time to 10 minutes and let cook until crispy and nicely golden brown.
- When cooked halfway, pull out fryer basket, shake mushrooms using tongs and insert basket back into the fryer until cooking time is over.
- Serve straight away.

Loaded Sweet Potato Wedges

| Servings: 2 |

| Preparation time: 15 minutes | Cooking time: 30 minutes | Total time: 45 minutes |

Ingredients:

- 2 medium organic sweet potatoes, peeled and rinsed
- 1 hard avocado, organic
- 2 tablespoons organic parsley, fresh
- 2 tablespoons organic cilantro, fresh
- 1/4 teaspoon garlic powder
- 1 teaspoon sea salt
- 2 teaspoons paprika
- 2 tablespoons avocado oil, pure
- 1 tablespoon crumbled Greek feta cheese, lactose-free
- Avocado wedges for serving

FOR THE SAUCE:
- 3 tablespoons avocado mayonnaise (homemade or Primal Kitchen)
- 1 tablespoon minced garlic, organic
- ¼ teaspoon ground black pepper, organic
- 1 tablespoons horseradish, sugar-free
- 2 tablespoons goat yogurt, lactose-free

Method:
- Cut sweet potatoes into thick wedges and place in a bowl.
- Add remaining ingredients, except for avocado and cheese, and toss to coat well.
- Switch on a 6-quarts air fryer, set temperature to 180 degrees C or 350 degrees F and time to 5 minutes to preheat it.
- Place wedges into the greased air fryer basket, insert into the air fryer, set frying time to 30 minutes and let cook until crispy and nicely browned.
- When cooked halfway, pull out fryer basket, shake wedges using tongs and insert basket back into the fryer until cooking time is over.
- In the meantime, prepare the sauce.

- For this, whisk together all the ingredients of sauce until well combined and then let cool in the refrigerator until required.
- When done, transfer wedges to a serving plate, top with avocado wedges, scatter with cheese and serve with prepared sauce.

Stuffed Portobello

| Servings: 1 |

| Preparation time: 10 minutes | Cooking time: 20 minutes | Total time: 30 minutes |

Ingredients:

- 1 large organic Portobello mushroom or 4 small organic mushrooms
- 1/2 teaspoon minced organic garlic
- 1 1/2 teaspoon dried parsley, organic
- ¼ teaspoon dried thyme, organic
- 3-ounce almond ricotta cheese, lactose-free

Method:
- Stir together garlic, parsley, thyme, and cheese until well mixed.
- Remove the stem of Portobello mushroom and then fill its cap with cheese mixture.
- Switch on a 6-quarts air fryer, set temperature to 199 degrees C or 390 degrees F and time to 5 minutes to preheat it.
- Place mushroom into a greased air fryer basket and insert it into the air fryer.
- Set frying time to 20 minutes and let cook until cooked through.
- Serve straight away.

Veggie Burger

| Servings: 4 burgers |
| Preparation time: 20 minutes | Cooking time: 31 minutes | Total time: 51 minutes |

Ingredients:

FOR THE PATTIES
- 2 cups walnuts
- 2 tablespoons cassava flour
- 2 cups chopped organic portobello mushrooms
- 2 cups cubed organic red beetroot
- ½ cup fresh basil, organic
- 2 tablespoons dried parsley, organic
- 1 cup chopped organic red onion
- 3 cloves of organic garlic, peeled
- 1 teaspoon salt
- ½ teaspoon ground black pepper, organic
- 1 teaspoon paprika, organic

FOR THE SAUCE
- 2 tablespoons horseradish, sugar-free
- ¼ teaspoon ground black pepper
- 1 tablespoon Kimchi Sriracha sauce, organic and sugar-free
- 1/2 teaspoon lemon juice, organic
- 2 tablespoons avocado mayonnaise

FOR THE BURGER
- 4 organic portobello mushrooms, stem removed
- 2 tablespoons avocado oil, pure
- ½ teaspoon salt
- ½ teaspoon ground black pepper, organic

Method:
- Place all the ingredients for patties in a food processor and process until minced.

- Then shape mixture into four patties, place into a greased air fryer basket and spray with oil.
- Switch on a 6-quarts air fryer, set temperature to 163 degrees C or 325 degrees F and time to 5 minutes to preheat it.
- Insert fryer basket into the air fryer, set frying time to 16 minutes and let cook until crispy and nicely browned.
- When cooked halfway, pull out fryer basket, turn using tongs and insert basket back into the fryer until cooking time is over.
- In the meantime, prepare the sauce.
- For this, whisk all the ingredients for the sauce, stir until combined and let cool in the refrigerator until required.
- When fryer beeps, transfer patties to a plate using tongs and keep them warm.
- Brush with oil, then season with salt and black pepper and add to fryer basket.
- Let cook for 15 minutes or until cooked through, turning mushrooms halfway through.
- To assemble burgers, place a patty over each mushroom, drizzle with prepared sauce, top with favorite topping and serve.

Cauliflower Tacos

| Servings: 4 |
| Preparation time: 10 minutes | Cooking time: 20 minutes | Total time: 30 minutes |

Ingredients:

- 1 medium head of organic cauliflower, cut into florets
- 5 red organic radishes, peeled and sliced
- 1 medium organic avocado, peeled, cored and sliced
- ½ cup organic cilantro, chopped
- 1/2 small organic jicama, grated
- 1/4 of a medium head of organic red cabbage, sliced thinly
- 1 teaspoon garlic powder, organic
- 1 ½ teaspoon salt
- 1 ¼ teaspoon ground black pepper, organic
- 3 tablespoons nutritional yeast, organic
- 1 tablespoon apple cider vinegar, organic
- 2 tablespoons organic lime juice, organic
- 5 tablespoons avocado oil, pure
- 4 Siete tortillas, organic

Method:
- Place cauliflower florets in a bowl, add garlic powder, 1 teaspoon salt, ¾ teaspoon black pepper, yeast, 3 tablespoons oil and toss to coat.
- Switch on a 6-quarts air fryer, set temperature to 191 degrees C or 375 degrees F and time to 5 minutes to preheat it.
- Add cauliflower florets into a greased air fryer basket and spread in a single layer.
- Insert fryer basket into the air fryer, set frying time to 22 minutes and let cook until crispy and nicely browned.
- When cooked halfway, pull out fryer basket, shake cauliflower florets using tongs and insert basket back into the fryer until cooking time is over.
- In the meantime, prepare the slaw.

- For this, place cabbage and jicama in a bowl, add vinegar along with remaining salt, black pepper, and oil.
- Toss to coat and then let rest in the refrigerator until required.
- Warm tortillas as well.
- To assemble tortillas, top with cauliflower and then with prepared slaw, drizzle with lime juice and wrap to serve.

Veggie Loaded Meatballs

| Servings: 12 balls |
| Preparation time: 15 minutes | Cooking time: 22 minutes | Total time: 37 minutes |

Ingredients:

- 12-ounce ground beef, grass-fed
- 8-ounce air-fryer purple sweet potato, mashed
- 1 stack of celery, organic
- 1 teaspoon salt
- 1 teaspoon ground black pepper, organic
- ¼ cup fresh cilantro, organic
- 1 tablespoon grated ginger, organic
- 1 teaspoon grated turmeric, organic
- 1 tablespoon minced garlic, organic
- 3 scallions, organic
- 1 egg, pasture raised
- 3 tablespoons cassava flour
- 2 tablespoons organic Kimchi Sriracha Sauce, organic
- 1 teaspoon toasted white sesame seeds, organic

Method:

- Place sweet potatoes, celery, cilantro, ginger, turmeric, garlic, scallions in a food processor and pulse until finely chopped.
- Tip the mixture into a bowl and add remaining ingredients except for sesame seeds and mix until well combined.
- Then shape mixture into 12 meatballs, then place them into an air fryer basket and grease with oil.
- Switch on a 6-quarts air fryer, set temperature to 180 degrees C or 350 degrees F and time to 5 minutes to preheat it.
- Insert fryer basket into the air fryer, set frying time to 22 minutes and let cook until cooked through and nicely browned.

- When cooked halfway, pull out fryer basket, shake meatballs using tongs and insert basket back into the fryer until cooking time is over.
- Garnish meatballs with sesame seeds and serve.

CHAPTER 8: POULTRY RECIPES

Sumac Chicken

| Servings: 6 |

| Preparation time: 1 hour and 5 minutes | Cooking time: 35 minutes | Total time: 1 hour and 40 minutes |

Ingredients:

- 4 pounds whole chicken, pasture raised
- 2 whole lemons, organic
- 2 teaspoons ground sumac
- 3 tablespoons minced garlic
- 2 teaspoons salt
- 1 tablespoon lemon juice, organic
- 1 teaspoon lemon zest
- 2 tablespoons olive oil

Method:
- Cut chicken into pieces and place in a large container.
- Rub generously with sumac, garlic, salt, lemon juice, lemon zest and oil and let marinate for 1 hour in the refrigerator.
- When ready to cook, switch on a 6-quarts air fryer, set temperature to 180 degrees C or 350 degrees F and time to 5 minutes to preheat it.
- Cut lemon into slices, arrange in the bottom of air fryer basket and top with marinated chicken pieces.
- Insert fryer basket into the air fryer, set frying time to 35 minutes and let cook until crispy and nicely golden brown.
- When cooked halfway, pull out fryer basket, turn chicken pieces using tongs and insert basket back into the fryer until cooking time is over.
- Serve when done.

Chicken Meatballs

| Servings: 4 |

| Preparation time: 15 minutes | Cooking time: 10 minutes | Total time: 25 minutes |

Ingredients:

- 1/2 cup almond flour
- 1 pound ground chicken
- 1 tablespoon fresh cilantro leaves, organic
- 1/2 cup chopped white onion, organic
- 3/4 teaspoon garlic powder, organic
- 1 teaspoon salt
- 3/4 teaspoon red chili powder, organic
- 1 cup organic teriyaki sauce, unsweetened
- 2 tablespoons sesame seeds

Method:
- Place all the ingredients in a bowl, except for sauce and sesame seeds, and stir until well combined.
- Then shape mixture into meatballs, about 18.
- Switch on a 6-quarts air fryer, set temperature to 180 degrees C or 350 degrees F and time to 5 minutes to preheat it.
- Place meatballs into greased air fryer basket in a single layer and then grease with cooking spray.
- Insert fryer basket into the air fryer, set frying time to 10 minutes and let cook until cooked through and nicely golden brown.
- When cooked halfway, pull out fryer basket, shake chicken using tongs and insert basket back into the fryer until cooking time is over.
- When done, transfer meatballs to a plate.
- Place a skillet pan over medium heat, add sauce and when heated through, add meatballs.
- Toss to coat, then sprinkle with sesame seed and serve.

Tarragon Chicken Salad

| Servings: 2 |

| Preparation time: 15 minutes | Cooking time: 8 minutes | Total time: 23 minutes |

Ingredients:

- 2 7-ounce chicken breasts, pasture raised
- 2 tablespoons avocado oil, pure
- 1 ½ teaspoon salt
- 1 ½ teaspoon ground black pepper
- 3 stacks of celery, chopped
- ¼ cup dry cranberries, unsweetened
- 2 tablespoons chopped tarragon
- 1 organic lemon, sliced
- 1 teaspoon lemon juice, organic
- 1/2 cup avocado mayonnaise

Method:

-
- Switch on a 6-quarts air fryer, set temperature to 238 degrees C or 460 degrees F and time to 5 minutes to preheat it.
- In the meantime, drizzle oil and lemon juice over chicken and season with 1 teaspoon each of salt and black pepper.
- Place lemon slices in the bottom of air fryer basket and top with chicken breasts.
- Insert fryer basket into the air fryer, set frying time to 8 minutes and let cook until cooked through and nicely golden browned.
- When cooked halfway, pull out fryer basket, turn chicken pieces using tongs and insert basket back into the fryer until cooking time is over.
- When fryer beeps, transfer to a cutting board, let cool for 10 minutes and then chop using a knife.
- To make a salad, place celery, cranberries, tarragon and stir until mixed.
- Add chicken, drizzle with mayonnaise, lemon juice and olive oil and season with remaining salt and black pepper.
- Toss until well mixed and serve.

Chicken Parmesan

| Servings: 4 |
| Preparation time: 15 minutes | Cooking time: 8 minutes | Total time: 23 minutes |

Ingredients:

- 4 chicken breast, pasture raised
- ½ cup coconut flour or almond flour
- 1/3 cup arrowroot flour
- 1 teaspoon garlic powder
- 1 teaspoon sea salt
- 1 teaspoon chopped basil
- 3 eggs, pasture raised
- ½ cup grated parmesan cheese, lactose-free
- ½ cup grated mozzarella cheese, lactose-free

Method:
- Pound each chicken breast using meat hammer until ½-inch thick.
- Stir together flour, garlic, salt and basil in a bowl until mixed.
- Crack eggs in another bowl and whisk slightly.
- Working on one chicken breast at a time, first dip into egg and then coat with flour mixture until coated.
- Then place coated chicken breast into an air fryer basket in a single layer and then grease with cooking spray.
- Switch on a 6-quarts air fryer, set temperature to 238 degrees C or 460 degrees F and time to 5 minutes to preheat it.
- Insert fryer basket into the air fryer, set frying time to 8 minutes and let cook until cooked through and nicely browned.
- When cooked halfway, pull out fryer basket, turn chicken using tongs and insert basket back into the fryer until cooking time is over.
- When done, top chicken breast evenly with cheeses and let cook for 1 to 2 minutes or until cheeses melt.
- Serve when ready.

Mustard Sage Chicken Wings

| Servings: 4 |
| Preparation time: 15 minutes | Cooking time: 24 minutes | Total time: 39 minutes |

Ingredients:

- 2 pounds chicken wings, pasture raised
- 1 teaspoon garlic powder, organic
- 1 teaspoon salt
- ½ teaspoon ground black pepper, organic
- 1 teaspoon dried sage, organic
- 1 teaspoon dried thyme, organic
- 1 tablespoon yellow mustard, organic

FOR MAYO DIPPING SAUCE:

- 1 teaspoon minced garlic, organic
- 1/2 teaspoon apple cider vinegar, organic
- 2 teaspoons olive oil
- 1/2 teaspoon lemon juice, organic
- 1/4 cup grated parmesan cheese, lactose-free
- 1/2 cups avocado mayonnaise

Method:

- Stir together garlic, salt, pepper, sage, thyme, and mustard until mixed.
- Rub this mixture over chicken wings, then place into a greased air fryer basket in a single layer, don't overcrowd the basket, and grease with cooking spray.
- Switch on a 6-quarts air fryer, set temperature to 190 degrees C or 380 degrees F and time to 5 minutes to preheat it.
- Insert fryer basket into the air fryer, set frying time to 24 minutes and let cook until crispy and nicely browned.
- When cooked halfway, pull out fryer basket, shake chicken wings using tongs and insert basket back into the fryer until cooking time is over.
- In the meantime, place all the ingredients for dip in a bowl and whisk until well combined.

- Cook remaining chicken wings in the same manner and serve with prepared dip and sweet potato fries.

Chicken Schnitzel

| Servings: 2 |
| Preparation time: 15 minutes | Cooking time: 11 minutes | Total time: 26 minutes |

Ingredients:

- 5 tablespoons almond flour
- 3 tablespoons cassava flour
- 4-ounce chicken breast, pasture raised
- ¾ teaspoon salt
- ½ teaspoon ground black pepper
- 1 egg, pasture raised

Method:

- Cut chicken into 3 equal slices and then pound using meat hammer into ½-inch thick.
- Crack an egg in a bowl and whisk in ¼ teaspoon each of salt and black pepper.
- Place flours in another bowl and stir in remaining salt and black pepper until mixed.
- First dip chicken pieces into egg mixture, then coat with flour mixture and place in a greased air fryer basket.
- Switch on a 6-quarts air fryer, set temperature to 199 degrees C or 390 degrees F and time to 5 minutes to preheat it.
- Insert fryer basket into the air fryer, set frying time to 11 minutes and let cook until crispy and nicely golden browned.
- When cooked halfway, pull out fryer basket, turn chicken pieces using tongs and insert basket back into the fryer until cooking time is over.
- Serve when ready.

Spinach Stuffed Chicken Breast

| Servings: 4 |
| Preparation time: 15 minutes | Cooking time: 30 minutes | Total time: 45 minutes |

Ingredients:

- 4 chicken breasts, pasture raised
- 4 cups chopped spinach, organic
- 1/4 teaspoon garlic powder, organic
- 1 teaspoon salt
- 1 teaspoon ground black pepper, organic
- 1 teaspoon dried oregano, organic
- 2 teaspoons paprika, organic
- 2 teaspoons Italian herbs mix, organic
- 3 tablespoons avocado mayonnaise
- 1 cup grated Pecorino Romano cheese, lactose-free

Method:
- Rinse spinach and let boil in boiling water for 3 to 4 minutes or until wilts.
- Then drain spinach and squeeze to drain excess water.
- Place spinach in a bowl, add mayonnaise and cheese and mix well until combined.
- Working on one chicken breast at a time, make a pocket into each chicken breast and then season the inside of the pocket with salt, black pepper, and Italian herbs.
- Then fill with spinach mixture until stuffed and close pocket with toothpicks.
- Switch on a 6-quarts air fryer, set temperature to 205 degrees C or 400 degrees F and time to 5 minutes to preheat it.
- Stuff remaining chicken breasts in the same manner and then season with garlic powder, salt, black pepper, oregano, and paprika.
- Place stuffed chicken breasts into greased air fryer basket in a single layer and then spray with cooking spray.
- Insert fryer basket into the air fryer, set frying time to 20 minutes and let cook until crispy and nicely browned.

- When cooked halfway, pull out fryer basket, turn chicken using tongs and insert basket back into the fryer until cooking time is over.
- Then lower cooking temperature to 375 degrees F and continue cooking for 10 minutes or until inserted meat thermometer into the chicken reads 165 degrees F.
- Serve when ready.

CHAPTER 9: PORK RECIPES

Pork Loin

| Servings: 8 |

| Preparation time: 15 minutes | Cooking time: 40 minutes | Total time: 55 minutes |

Ingredients:

- 4 pounds pastured pork loin, fat trimmed
- 2 ½ teaspoon garlic salt
- 1 teaspoon ground black pepper, organic
- 4 teaspoons dried marjoram, organic
- 1 1/2 teaspoons summer savory, organic
- 1/4 teaspoon dried rosemary, organic
- 4 teaspoons dried thyme, organic
- 1/4 teaspoon dried mint, organic
- 1/8 teaspoon dried sage, organic
- ¼ cup avocado oil, pure

Method:
- Cut pork in halved, then brush generously with oil and coat with remaining ingredients.
- Switch on a 6-quarts air fryer, set temperature to 182 degrees C or 360 degrees F and time to 5 minutes to preheat it.
- Place pork into an air fryer basket, then insert it into the air fryer, set frying time to 25 minutes and let cook.
- Then turn pork and continue air frying for 15 minutes or until meat thermometer inserted into pork reads 145 degrees F.
- Slice to serve.

Pork Schnitzel

| Servings: 4 |
| Preparation time: 15 minutes | Cooking time: 12 minutes | Total time: 27 minutes |

Ingredients:

- 4 3-ounce pork cutlets, pastured
- 1/4 cup almond flour
- 1 tablespoon tapioca flour
- ¼ teaspoon salt
- ¼ teaspoon cayenne pepper, organic
- ½ teaspoon dried oregano, organic
- 2 eggs, pasture raised

Method:
- Pound pork cutlets with a meat hammer until ¼ inch thick.
- Crack an egg in a bowl and whisk.
- Stir together remaining ingredients in another bowl until mixed.
- First, dip pork cutlet into the egg, then coat with flour mixture and place in a greased air frying basket.
- Fill the basket with more coated pork cutlets, don't overcrowd the basket and spray with oil.
- Switch on a 6-quarts air fryer, set temperature to 205 degrees C or 400 degrees F and time to 5 minutes to preheat it.
- Insert fryer basket into the air fryer, set frying time to 12 minutes and let cook until cooked through and nicely browned.
- When cooked halfway, pull out fryer basket, turn pork using tongs and insert basket back into the fryer until cooking time is over.
- Serve when ready.

Parmesan Crusted Pork

| Servings: 6 |
| Preparation time: 15 minutes | Cooking time: 15 minutes | Total time: 30 minutes |

Ingredients:

- 6 boneless pork chops, pastured
- 1 cup almond meal
- 1/2 teaspoon onion powder
- 1 teaspoon sea salt
- 1/4 teaspoon ground black pepper
- 1/4 teaspoon red chili powder
- 1 teaspoon smoked paprika
- 3 tablespoons grated parmesan cheese, lactose-free
- 2 eggs

Method:

- Place almond meal in a bowl and stir in black pepper, red chili powder, paprika, and cheese until mixed.
- Crack eggs in another bowl and whisk.
- First dip pork in egg, then coat with almond meal mixture and place in a greased air fryer basket.
- Coat remaining pork chops in the same manner and add to fryer basket in a single layer, don't overcrowd the basket.
- Switch on a 6-quarts air fryer, set temperature to 205 degrees C or 400 degrees F and time to 5 minutes to preheat it.
- Insert fryer basket into the air fryer, set frying time to 15 minutes and let cook until crispy and nicely browned.
- When cooked halfway, pull out fryer basket, turn pork chops using tongs and insert basket back into the fryer until cooking time is over.
- When fryer beeps, transfer pork chops to a plate and cook remaining pork chops in the same manner.
- Serve immediately.

Pork Belly

| Servings: 6 |

| Preparation time: 10 minutes | Cooking time: 45 minutes | Total time: 55 minutes |

Ingredients:

- 2 pounds pork belly, pastured
- 1 teaspoon sea salt
- 1 tablespoon avocado oil, pure

Method:

- Score pork meat roughly, at 1 cm intervals, then pat dry with paper towels until dry completely.
- Rub with oil, then season with salt and place belly into a greased air fryer basket.
- Switch on a 6-quarts air fryer, set temperature to 94 degrees C or 200 degrees F and time to 5 minutes to preheat it.
- Insert fryer basket into the air fryer, set frying time to 30 minutes and let cook until crispy and nicely browned.
- When cooked halfway, pull out fryer basket, turn belly using tongs and insert basket back into the fryer until cooking time is over.
- Then lower cooking temperature to 190 degrees F and continue air frying for 15 minutes.
- When fryer beeps, transfer pork belly to a cutting board and let rest for 10 minutes.
- Slice to serve.

Bone-in Pork Chops

| Servings: 6 |
| Preparation time: 10 minutes | Cooking time: 20 minutes | Total time: 30 minutes |

Ingredients:

- 6 bone-in pork chops, pastured
- 1/2 teaspoon garlic powder, organic
- 1 tablespoon salt
- ¾ teaspoon ground black pepper, organic
- ½ teaspoon Italian herb seasoning, organic
- 2 tablespoons avocado oil

Method:

- Coat pork chops with oil and then rub with garlic powder, salt, black pepper and Italian seasoning.
- Switch on a 6-quarts air fryer, set temperature to 190 degrees C or 380 degrees F and time to 5 minutes to preheat it.
- Place pork chops into a greased air fryer basket in a single layer, then insert basket into air fryer and set frying time to 15 minutes.
- Then pull out fryer basket, turn pork chops using tongs, insert basket back into the fryer and continue cooking for 5 minutes or until cooked through.
- Serve straight away.

Char Siu Pork

| Servings: 8 |

| Preparation time: 50 minutes | Cooking time: 30 minutes | Total time: 1 hour and 20 minutes |

Ingredients:

- 1 pound pork shoulder, pastured
- 4 tablespoons organic plum jam, unsweetened
- ½ teaspoon ginger powder, organic
- 4 tablespoons erythritol
- ½ teaspoon Chinese five spice powder, organic
- ½ teaspoon Red Boat fish sauce, organic and unsweetened
- 1 ½ tablespoons tomato paste, organic
- ½ tablespoon almond butter

Method:

- Place all the ingredients in a pan, except for pork and whisk until mixed.
- Place pan over medium heat and bring sauce to simmer, whisking frequently.
- Then remove the pan from heat and let sauce completely.
- In the meantime, cut pork into ½ inch thick slices, pierce with a fork and then place slices in a plastic bag.
- Add half of the cooled sauce, let seal plastic bag and turn it upside down to coat well.
- Let pork marinate for 30 minutes and then transfer to a greased air fryer basket in a single layer, don't overcrowd the basket.
- Switch on a 6-quarts air fryer, set temperature to 199 degrees C or 390 degrees F and time to 5 minutes to preheat it.
- Insert fryer basket into the air fryer, set frying time to 15 minutes and let cook until crispy and nicely browned.
- When cooked halfway, pull out fryer basket, turn pork using tongs, baste with reserved sauce and insert basket back into the fryer until cooking time is over.
- When pork is cooked and brush again.
- Slice pork sauce and serve with cauliflower fried rice.

Pork Chops

| Servings: 6 |

| Preparation time: 10 minutes | Cooking time: 20 minutes | Total time: 30 minutes |

Ingredients:

- 6 pork chops, pastured
- 1/2 cup almond meal
- 2 eggs, pasture raised
- 2 teaspoons onion powder, organic
- 2 teaspoons garlic powder, organic
- 1 teaspoon sea salt
- 2 teaspoons ground black pepper, organic
- 1 teaspoon red chili powder, organic
- 1 teaspoon paprika, organic
- 2 teaspoons fresh parsley, organic

Method:
- Place all the ingredients, except for pork chops and eggs, in a large plastic bag seal the bag and shake until mixed.
- Crack eggs in a bowl, whisk slightly and dip a pork chop in it.
- Drop this into the plastic bag, seal the bag, turn it upside down to coat pork chops completely and transfer this pork chop into a greased air fryer basket.
- Coat remaining pork chops, at a time, in the same manner, and add to fryer basket in a single layer, don't overcrowd the pan.
- Switch on a 6-quarts air fryer, set temperature to 191 degrees C or 375 degrees F and time to 5 minutes to preheat it.
- Spray oil over pork chops, then insert fryer basket into the air fryer, set frying time to 16 minutes and let cook until cooked through and nicely golden brown.
- When cooked halfway, pull out fryer basket, turn pork chops using tongs and insert basket back into the fryer until cooking time is over.
- Cook remaining pork chops in the same manner and serve straight away.

CHAPTER 10: BEEF RECIPES

Meatloaf

| Servings: 12 |

| Preparation time: 15 minutes | Cooking time: 25 minutes | Total time: 40 minutes |

Ingredients:

- 16-ounce ground beef, grass-fed
- 6 tablespoons cassava flour
- 1 small organic sweet potato, peeled and grated
- 1 small organic carrot, grated
- 2 big stacks of organic celery, chopped
- 3 cups baby spinach, organic
- 1 medium yellow onion, peeled and chopped
- 1 teaspoon salt
- 1 teaspoon ground black pepper, organic
- 2 tablespoons dried parsley, organic
- 1 tablespoon dried oregano, organic
- 1/2 tablespoon dried thyme, organic
- 2 tablespoons avocado oil, pure
- 1 egg, pasture raized

Method:
- Place a skillet pan over medium heat, add oil and when heated, add onion and celery.
- Let sauté for 5 to 7 minutes or until soft and then add spinach.
- Let spinach cook for 4 minutes or until leaves wilt and then stir in carrot and sweet potatoes.
- Continue cooking for 2 minutes, then transfer mixture to a bowl and let cool completely.
- Add remaining ingredients and stir until well combined.

- Spoon this meatloaf mixture into an air fryer baking pan, smooth the top using spatula and grease top with oil.
- Switch on a 6-quarts air fryer, set temperature to 200 degrees C or 392 degrees F and time to 5 minutes to preheat it.
- Insert fryer pan into the air fryer, set frying time to 25 minutes and let cook until top is nicely browned, and meatloaf is cooked through.
- When fryer beeps, take out the pan from the air fryer and carefully pull out meatloaf.
- Let meatloaf rest for 10 minutes and then slice to serve.

Italian Meatballs

| Servings: 6 |
| Preparation time: 15 minutes | Cooking time: 24 minutes | Total time: 39 minutes |

Ingredients:

- 1 tablespoon cassava flour and more for coating meatballs
- 16-ounces ground beef, grass fed
- 5 medium button mushrooms, organic
- 1 cup parsley, organic
- ½ cup basil leaves, organic
- 1 large organic white onion, peeled
- 3 cloves of garlic, organic
- 1 teaspoon salt
- ¾ teaspoon ground black pepper, organic
- 1 teaspoon dried oregano, organic
- 2 eggs, pasture raised

Method:

- Place mushroom, parsley, basil, onion, and garlic in a food processor and pulse at high speed for 1 to 2 minutes or until chopped.
- Tip this mixture in a bowl, add remaining ingredients and stir until well combined.
- Then shape mixture into meatballs, coat with flour, place into an air fryer basket in a single layer and coat meatballs with cooking spray.
- Switch on a 6-quarts air fryer, set temperature to 205 degrees C or 400 degrees F and time to 5 minutes to preheat it.
- Insert fryer basket into the air fryer, set frying time to 12 minutes and let cook until meatballs are nicely browned and cooked through.
- When cooked halfway, pull out fryer basket, shake meatballs using tongs and insert basket back into the fryer until cooking time is over.
- When fryer beeps, transfer meatballs to a plate and cook remaining meatballs in the same manner.
- Serve when ready.

Beef Roast

| Servings: 6 |
| Preparation time: 10 minutes | Cooking time: 15 minutes | Total time: 25 minutes |

Ingredients:

- 2 pounds grass-fed beef roast, fat trimmed
- 1 tablespoon garlic salt
- 1 tablespoon dried thyme
- 1 teaspoon ground black pepper
- ½ cup Worcestershire sauce

Method:

- Place roast in a bowl, add remaining ingredients and let coat completely.
- Switch on a 6-quarts air fryer, set temperature to 180 degrees C or 350 degrees F and time to 5 minutes to preheat it.
- Brush chicken with olive oil and place them in a single layer into the fryer basket, greased with non-stick cooking spray.
- Place beef roast into air fryer basket, then insert it into the air fryer and set frying time to 15 minutes.
- Let cook until roast is medium-rare, cook more according to the desired doneness.
- When cooked halfway, pull out fryer basket, turn roast using tongs and insert basket back into the fryer until cooking time is over.
- When fryer beeps, transfer roast to a plate and let cool for 10 minutes.
- Slice to serve.

Mexican Steak

| Servings: 4 |
| Preparation time: 10 minutes | Cooking time: 12 minutes | Total time: 22 minutes |

Ingredients:

- 2 pounds sirloin steak, grass-fed
- 1/8 teaspoon salt
- 1/4 teaspoon ground black pepper, organic
- 1 tablespoon red chili powder, organic
- 1/4 teaspoon cayenne pepper, organic
- 1 tablespoon paprika, organic
- 1/2 tablespoon dried oregano, organic
- 1/2 tablespoon ground cumin, organic
- 1/2 teaspoon dry mustard, organic

Method:

- Switch on a 6-quarts air fryer, set temperature to 205 degrees C or 400 degrees F and time to 5 minutes to preheat it.
- In the meantime, place all the ingredients except for steaks in a large bowl and stir until mixed.
- Add steak and rub this seasoning generously.
- Place steaks into frying basket in a single layer, spray with oil and insert it into the air fryer.
- Set frying time to 12 minutes and let cook until cooked through and nicely browned.
- When cooked halfway, pull out fryer basket, turn steaks using tongs and insert basket back into the fryer until cooking time is over.
- Cook remaining steaks in the same manner and serve with guacamole.

Mongolian Beef

| Servings: 4 |
| Preparation time: 15 minutes | Cooking time: 10 minutes | Total time: 25 minutes |

Ingredients:

- 1 pound flank steak, grass-fed cut into 1/4-inch thick pieces against the grain
- 2 teaspoons almond meal, organic
- 2 tablespoons minced garlic, organic
- 2 teaspoons grated ginger, organic
- 1/2 cup erythritol
- ½ cup soy sauce, organic
- 2 teaspoon sesame oil, pure
- ½ cup water

Method:

- Switch on a 6-quarts air fryer, set temperature to 199 degrees C or 390 degrees F and time to 5 minutes to preheat it.
- Cut steak into ¼-inch pieces, then coat with almond meal and place into greased fryer basket.
- Insert fryer basket into the air fryer, set frying time to 10 minutes and let cook until done.
- When cooked halfway, pull out fryer basket, shake beef using tongs and insert basket back into the fryer until cooking time is over.
- In the meantime, whisk together remaining ingredients until well combined and pour this sauce into a pan.
- Place pan over medium-low heat and bring sauce to a low boil, then set aside until required.
- When fryer beeps, transfer beef to sauce and let soak for 10 minutes.
- Then remove beef from sauce using tongs, garnish with scallion and serve with vegetables and cauliflower fried rice.

Beef Empanadas

| Servings: 6 |
| Preparation time: 45 minutes | Cooking time: 16 minutes | Total time: 1 hour and 1 minute |

Ingredients:

FOR CRUST
- 2 cups almond meal
- 1/2 cup tapioca flour
- 1/4 teaspoon baking soda, organic
- 1 teaspoon sea salt
- 3 tablespoons avocado oil, pure
- 2 eggs, pasture raised
- Coconut flour for dusting

FOR BEEF EMPANADAS
- 1 pound ground beef, grass-fed
- 3-ounces green chilies, drained and chopped
- 2 medium organic tomatoes, seeded and diced
- 1/2 of medium organic yellow onion, peeled and chopped
- 1 teaspoon minced garlic, organic
- 1 teaspoon sea salt
- 1 teaspoon cayenne pepper
- 1 teaspoon ground cumin
- 2 tablespoons avocado oil, pure
- 1 egg, pasture raised

Method:
- First prepare pastry, for this, place flour in a bowl and stir in baking soda and salt until combined.
- Crack eggs in another bowl, whisk slightly and then whisk into flour mixture until incorporated.

- Mix in oil, then shape mixture into a dough, cover it with plastic wrap and let refrigerator for 30 minutes.
- In the meantime, cook beef.
- For this, place a skillet pan over medium heat, add oil and when heated, add onion and garlic.
- Let cook for 5 minutes or until tender.
- Then stir in chilies, tomatoes, salt, cumin and cayenne pepper along with beef.
- Continue cooking for 25 minutes or until all the cooking liquid gets evaporated, covering the pan and stirring occasionally.
- Remove pan from heat when done.
- Uncover pastry dough, place it on a clean working space, dust with coconut flour and divide evenly into 10 pieces.
- Roll each piece into a 6-inch circle with a rolling pin.
- Working on one empanada at a time, place 3 tablespoons of beef mixture on one half of circle and then fold over another half of circle.
- Seal by pressing edges using a fork and prepare remaining empanada in the same manner.
- Switch on a 6-quarts air fryer, set temperature to 163 degrees C or 325 degrees F and time to 5 minutes to preheat it.
- In the meantime, whisk the egg and brush on pastry generously and place pastry into a greased air fryer basket, don't overcrowd the basket.
- Insert fryer basket into the air fryer, set frying time to 8 minutes and let cook until top is nicely browned.
- When cooked halfway, pull out fryer basket, turn pastry using tongs and insert basket back into the fryer until cooking time is over.
- Cook remaining empanada in the same manner and serve.

Beef & Veggies Stir-Fry

| Servings: 6 |
| Preparation time: 25 minutes | Cooking time: 11 minutes | Total time: 36 minutes |

Ingredients:

- 1 pound beef steak, grass-fed
- 1 medium organic green bell pepper, cored and cut into strips
- 2 medium organic carrots, peeled and sliced
- 1 head of small organic napa cabbage, sliced
- 3 organic scallions, minced and more for garnishing
- 1 tablespoon grated ginger, organic
- 2 teaspoons minced garlic, organic
- 2 teaspoons erythritol
- 2 teaspoons lime juice, organic
- 2 tablespoons avocado oil

FOR THE SAUCE
- ¼ cup of hoisin sauce, organic
- 2 teaspoons minced garlic, organic
- 1 teaspoon of sesame oil
- 1 tablespoon soy sauce, organic
- 1 teaspoon grated ginger, organic
- ¼ cup of water

Method:
- Place all the ingredients for sauce in a bowl and whisk until combined.
- Cut beef into strips, add to bowl, toss to coat and let marinate for 20 minutes in the refrigerator.
- In the meantime, switch on a 6-quarts air fryer, set the temperature to 94 degrees C or 200 degrees F and time to 5 minutes to preheat it.
- Place prepared vegetable in a bowl, add oil and toss to coat.
- Add vegetables to fryer basket, insert it into the air fryer, set frying time to 5 minutes and let cook until softened.

- Then pull out fryer basket, shake vegetables using tongs and if vegetables aren't tender, air fry for another 2 minutes.
- When done, transfer vegetables to a bowl and add marinated beef into the fryer basket.
- Increase air fryer cooking temperature to 360 degrees F and let beef cook for 6 minutes or until cooked through, turning beef halfway through.
- Serve beef and vegetables together.

Steak Fajitas

| Servings: 4 |
| Preparation time: 10 minutes | Cooking time: 10 minutes | Total time: 20 minutes |

Ingredients:

- 1 pound beef steak, cut into strips
- 1/2 of a medium purple onion, peeled and sliced
- 1 medium green bell pepper, cored and sliced
- 1 medium red bell pepper, cored and sliced
- 1/2 of a medium yellow onion, peeled and sliced
- 1/4 teaspoon garlic powder, organic
- 2 teaspoons salt
- 1 teaspoon ground black pepper, organic
- 1/4 teaspoon red chili powder, organic
- 1/4 teaspoon dried oregano
- 1/2 ground cumin, organic
- 2 tablespoons avocado oil

Method:
- Stir together garlic, salt, black pepper, chili powder, oregano, cumin and oil until combined.
- Add remaining ingredients and toss until well coated.
- Switch on a 6-quarts air fryer, set temperature to 199 degrees C or 390 degrees F and time to 5 minutes to preheat it.
- In the meantime, line air fryer basket with parchment sheet and add seasoned vegetables and beef.
- Insert fryer basket into the air fryer, set frying time to 10 minutes and let cook until crispy and nicely browned.
- When cooked halfway, pull out fryer basket, shake vegetables and beef using tongs and insert basket back into the fryer until cooking time is over.
- Serve when done.

CHAPTER 11: SEAFOOD & FISH RECIPES

Mexican Tuna Steak with Avocado Salsa

| Servings: 2 |
| Preparation time: 5 minutes | Cooking time: 8 minutes | Total time: 13 minutes |

Ingredients:

- 2 wild caught tuna steaks, 1-cm thick
- 1/8 teaspoon sea salt
- 1/8 teaspoon ground black pepper, organic
- 1 teaspoon ground coriander, organic
- 1 organic lime, zested
- 1 tablespoon avocado oil, pure

FOR SALSA
- 1 large organic avocado, peeled, cored and chopped
- 2 tablespoon chopped coriander, organic
- 1/8 teaspoon sea salt
- 1 tablespoon organic lime juice

Method:
- Switch on a 6-quarts air fryer, set temperature to 199 degrees C or 390 degrees F and time to 5 minutes to preheat it.
- In the meantime, stir together remaining ingredients in a bowl, add tuna steaks and toss until well coated.
- Place tuna steaks into air fryer basket, then insert it into the air fryer and set frying time to 8 minutes.
- Let cook until tuna turns crispy and nicely browned and shake tuna using tongs halfway through.
- In the meantime, place avocado flesh in a bowl, add coriander and mash using a fork.
- Then stir in salt and lime juice and set aside until tuna is ready.

- When fryer beeps, transfer tuna steaks to a plate and serve with prepared avocado salsa.

Crab Cakes

| Servings: 7 cakes |
| Preparation time: 10 minutes | Cooking time: 20 minutes | Total time: 30 minutes |

Ingredients:

- 12 ounce wild caught crab lump
- 5 tbsp Tigernut flour
- ¼ tablespoon salt
- ¼ tablespoon ground black pepper, organic
- ¼ tablespoon paprika, organic
- ¼ tablespoon garam masala, organic
- ¼ tablespoon allspice, organic
- ¼ tablespoon ground nutmeg, organic
- ¼ cup chopped parsley, organic
- 1 tablespoon mustard, grain-free
- 2 tablespoons mayonnaise, lactose-free
- 2 eggs, pasture raised

Method:
- Place all the ingredients in a large bowl and stir until mixed.
- Then shape mixture into 7 patties and set aside until ready to cook.
- Switch on a 6-quarts air fryer, set temperature to 199 degrees C or 390 degrees F and time to 5 minutes to preheat it.
- Brush patties with oil and place them in a single layer into the fryer basket, greased with non-stick cooking spray.
- Insert fryer basket into the air fryer, set frying time to 20 minutes and let cook until crispy and nicely browned.
- When cooked halfway, pull out fryer basket, shake cakes using tongs and insert basket back into the fryer until cooking time is over.
- When fryer beeps, transfer cakes to serving platter using tongs and cook remaining cakes in the same manner.
- Serve straight away.

Shrimp Tostadas

| Servings: 4 Tostadas |

| Preparation time: 10 minutes | Cooking time: 20 minutes | Total time: 30 minutes |

Ingredients:

- 2 cups wild caught shrimps, peeled and deveined
- 1/2 of small red cabbage, thinly sliced
- 1 medium avocado, peeled, cored and sliced
- 4 slices of scallions, chopped
- 1 cup chopped cilantro, organic
- 1 tablespoon minced garlic, organic
- 1/2 teaspoon salt
- 1/2 teaspoon ground black pepper, organic
- 1/2 teaspoon ground cumin, organic
- 1 teaspoon dried oregano, organic
- 1/4 teaspoon cayenne pepper, organic
- 4 tablespoons nutritional yeast
- 5 tablespoons organic lime juice
- 2 tablespoons avocado oil, pure
- 4 almond flour tortillas

Method:

- Place cleaned shrimps in a bowl, add garlic, ¼ teaspoon each of salt and black pepper, cumin, oregano, cayenne pepper, oil and 4 tablespoons lime juice.
- Stir until well combined and let marinate in the refrigerator for 30 minutes.
- Switch on a 6-quarts air fryer, set temperature to 163 degrees C or 325 degrees F and time to 5 minutes to preheat it.
- Add marinated shrimps to greased fryer basket, then insert it into the air fryer and set frying time to 10 minutes.
- Let fry until crispy and cooked through and shake shrimps using tongs halfway through frying.

- In the meantime, slice avocado, then season with remaining salt and black pepper and drizzle with remaining lime juice and set aside until required.
- Warm tortillas in a skillet pan.
- When fryer beeps, transfer shrimps to a plate and start assembling Tostadas.
- For this, place a tortilla on a clean working space, spread cabbage on top along with shrimps.
- Sprinkle with cilantro, top with avocado and green onion, then sprinkle with yeast and wrap it.
- Prepare remaining Tostadas in the same manner and serve.

Salmon & Prosciutto Mini Pizzas

| Servings: 4 |
| Preparation time: 20 minutes | Cooking time: 60 minutes | Total time: 1 hour and 20 minutes |

Ingredients:

- 4 Prosciutto di Parma
- 6 ounce wild caught salmon, air fried and sliced
- 4 tablespoons sliced green olives, organic
- ½ cup sliced red pickled onions, organic
- 1 tablespoon dried oregano, organic
- 2 tablespoons capers, organic
- 2 tablespoons chopped tarragon, organic
- 2 tablespoons Kimchi-Sriracha sauce, organic
- 2 tablespoons avocado oil, pure
- 4 bocconcini buffalo mozzarella cheese, grass fed
- 12 ounce prepared pizza dough, low-lectin compliant

Method:

- Place dough on a clean working space, divide into four portions and then flatten each portion into a thin crust using a rolling pin.
- Switch on a 6-quarts air fryer, set temperature to 163 degrees C or 325 degrees F and time to 5 minutes to preheat it.
- Brush air fryer baking pan with oil and place one pizza dough in it, add another if there is more space.
- Insert baking pan into the air fryer, set frying time to 7 minutes and let cooktop is nicely browned.
- In the meantime, cut cheese and pat dry with paper towels until dry.
- When air fryer beef, remove baking pan from oven and scatter with half of the salmon slices, ½ tablespoon each of capers and tarragon, 1 mozzarella cheese and 1 tablespoon olives.

- Return baking pan into the air fryer and continue frying for 8 minutes or until crust is cooked through and pizza edges turn brown and crispy.
- When done, carefully remove pizza from pan, drizzle with oil and ½ tablespoon hot sauce, and sprinkle with oregano.
- Prepare another pizza with remaining salmon pieces and other two pizza with Prosciutto slices.
- Serve warm.

Salmon with Lime and Rosemary

| Servings: 2 |
| Preparation time: 5 minutes | Cooking time: 10 minutes | Total time: 15 minutes |

Ingredients:

- 2 wild caught salmon filets
- 1/4 teaspoon sea salt
- 1/8 teaspoon ground black pepper, organic
- 1 tablespoon fresh rosemary, organic
- 1 tablespoon organic lime juice
- 3 tablespoon avocado oil, pure

Method:

- Switch on a 6-quarts air fryer, set temperature to 205 degrees C or 400 degrees F and time to 5 minutes to preheat it.
- In the meantime, place all the ingredients except for salmon in a bowl and stir until mixed.
- Add salmon and toss to coat and then place fillets into a greased air fryer basket.
- Insert fryer basket into the air fryer, set frying time to 10 minutes and let fry until crispy and nicely browned.
- When cooked halfway, pull out fryer basket, shake fillets using tongs and insert basket back into the fryer until cooking time is over.
- When fryer beeps, transfer salmon fillets to a plate and serve.

Fish & Sweet Potato Chips

| Servings: 4 |

| Preparation time: 10 minutes | Cooking time: 10 minutes | Total time: 20 minutes |

Ingredients:

- 1 pound wild caught cod
- 1 cup of almond flour
- 1 teaspoon sea salt
- 2 eggs, pasture raised
- 1/2 cup coconut milk, unsweetened
- Crispy sweet potato chips for serving

Method:
- Place flour in a food processor and add salt, eggs, and milk.
- Pulse at high speed until smooth and then tip mixture in a large bowl.
- Add cod and toss to coat and place in a greased fryer basket.
- Switch on a 6-quarts air fryer, set temperature to 205 degrees C or 400 degrees F and time to 5 minutes to preheat it.
- Then insert fryer basket into the air fryer, set frying time to 10 minutes and let fry until crispy and nicely browned.
- When cooked halfway, pull out fryer basket, shake cod using tongs and insert basket back into the fryer until cooking time is over.
- When fryer beeps, transfer cod to a plate and serve
- Serve straight away.

Hot Prawns

| Servings: 6 |
| Preparation time: 5 minutes | Cooking time: 8 minutes | Total time: 14 minutes |

Ingredients:

- 12 king prawns, fresh
- 1 teaspoon sea salt
- ½ teaspoon ground black pepper, organic
- 1 teaspoon red chili powder, organic
- 1 teaspoon red chili flakes, organic

Method:

- Switch on a 6-quarts air fryer, set temperature to 199 degrees C or 390 degrees F and time to 5 minutes to preheat it.
- In the meantime, place all the ingredients except for prawns in a bowl and stir until mixed.
- Add prawns, toss to coat and then add to a greased air fryer basket.
- Insert fryer basket into the air fryer, set frying time to 8 minutes and let fry until crispy and nicely browned.
- When cooked halfway, pull out fryer basket, shake prawns using tongs and insert basket back into the fryer until cooking time is over.
- When fryer beeps, transfer prawns to a plate platter using tongs and serve.

Fried Red Snapper

| Servings: 6 |
| Preparation time: 10 minutes | Cooking time: 16 minutes | Total time: 26 minutes |

Ingredients:

- 6 pieces of wild caught red snapper, cleaned
- 1 teaspoon onion powder, organic
- 1 teaspoon garlic powder, organic
- 1 ½ teaspoon sea salt
- ½ teaspoon ground black pepper, organic
- ¼ teaspoon dried rosemary, organic
- ¼ teaspoon ground cumin, organic
- ¼ teaspoon ground coriander, organic
- ½ cup apple cider vinegar, organic
- ½ teaspoon organic lime juice

Method:
- Place fish in a bowl, add vinegar, let soak for 5 minutes and then rinse fish thoroughly.
- Place remaining ingredients except for oil in a bowl and stir until smooth paste comes together.
- Add fish pieces, toss to coat and then place in a greased air fryer basket.
- Switch on a 6-quarts air fryer, set temperature to 199 degrees C or 390 degrees F and time to 5 minutes to preheat it.
- Insert fryer basket into the air fryer, set frying time to 16 minutes and let fry until crispy and nicely browned.
- When cooked halfway, pull out fryer basket, turn fish pieces using tongs and insert basket back into the fryer until cooking time is over.
- When fryer beeps, transfer fish to a plate and serve.

CHAPTER 12: SWEET RECIPES

Apple Chips

| Servings: 2 |
| Preparation time: 5 minutes | Cooking time: 8 minutes | Total time: 12 minutes |

Ingredients:

- 1 organic apple, peeled and cored
- 1/8 teaspoon salt
- 1 tablespoon erythritol
- 1/2 teaspoon ground cinnamon, organic

Method:

- Switch on a 6-quarts air fryer, set temperature to 199 degrees C or 390 degrees F and time to 5 minutes to preheat it.
- In the meantime, peel and core the apple and cut into thin slices horizontally.
- Stir together salt, sugar, and cinnamon in a large bowl until mix, then add slices of apples and toss until well coated.
- Place these apple slices in a single layer into the fryer basket, greased with non-stick cooking spray.
- Insert fryer basket into the air fryer, set frying time to 8 minutes and let cook until nicely browned.
- When cooked halfway, pull out fryer basket, shake apple slices using tongs and insert basket back into the fryer until cooking time is over.
- When fryer beeps, transfer apple slice to a bowl using tongs and cook remaining apple slices in the same manner.
- Let apple chips cool slightly before serving.

Carrot Cake

| Servings: 1 cake |
| Preparation time: 15 minutes | Cooking time: 10 minutes | Total time: 25 minutes |

Ingredients:

- 1 cup grated organic carrots, peeled
- 1 cup almond flour, blanched
- 3 tablespoons coconut flour
- 2/3 teaspoon baking soda
- 1/2 teaspoon ginger powder, organic
- 1/8 teaspoon salt
- 4 tablespoons erythritol
- 1 1/2 teaspoon ground cinnamon, organic
- 1/4 teaspoon ground nutmeg, organic
- 2 teaspoons vanilla extract, unsweetened
- 3 tablespoons walnuts, powdered
- 2 ½ tablespoons pecans, powdered
- 1/4 cup shredded coconut, unsweetened
- 1/3 cup avocado oil, pure
- 2 eggs pasture, raised
- 2/3 cup coconut milk, unsweetened

Method:
- Place flours in a large bowl and stir baking soda, ginger powder, salt, cinnamon, nutmeg, almond until well mixed.
- Crack eggs in another bowl and blend in erythritol, vanilla, oil, and milk until well blended.
- Gradually stir this mixture into flour mixture until incorporated and then fold in carrots, and pecans until mixed.
- Switch on a 6-quarts air fryer, set temperature to 180 degrees C or 355 degrees F and time to 5 minutes to preheat it.

- Take a cake tin, large enough to fit into air fryer basket, line it with baking sheet and spoon in the prepared cake batter, smoothing the top with a spatula.
- Place cake tin into the air fryer basket and insert it into air fryer, then set cooking time to 5 minutes and let cook until crispy and nicely browned.
- After 5 minutes, lower cooking temperature to 160 degrees C or 320 degrees F and continue cooking for another 5 minutes.
- Check for cake doneness using a toothpick which should come out from the cake clean.
- When fryer beeps, remove cake tin from the air fryer and let it cool for 10 minutes.
- Take out the cake from the tin, sprinkle with shredded coconut and slice to serve.

Lemon Raspberry Muffins

| Servings: 6 muffins |
| Preparation time: 10 minutes | Cooking time: 15 minutes | Total time: 25 minutes |

Ingredients:

- ½ cup raspberries, organic
- ¾ cup almond flour, blanched
- 2 tablespoons coconut flour
- ¼ teaspoon salt
- 3 tablespoons erythritol
- ½ teaspoon baking soda
- 1 teaspoon vanilla extract, unsweetened
- 2 organic lemons, juiced and zested
- 1/4 cup avocado oil, pure
- 3 eggs, pasture raised
- 1/4 cup coconut milk, unsweetened

Method:

- Place flours in a bowl and stir in salt and baking soda until mixed.
- Crack eggs in another bowl and whisk in erythritol, vanilla, lemon juice and zest, oil, and milk until blended.
- Gradually this mixture into flour mixture until incorporated and then fold in berries until just mixed.
- Switch on a 6-quarts air fryer, set temperature to 160 degrees C or 320 degrees F and time to 5 minutes to preheat it.
- In the meantime, spoon muffin batter evenly into six cupcake holders using an ice cream scoop.
- Place cupcakes into the air fryer basket and insert it into air fryer, then set frying time to 15 minutes and let cook until muffin raised, and the top is nicely golden brown.
- Check your muffin doneness by inserting a wooden skewer into them which should come out clean.

- When fryer beeps, take out muffins from air fryer and let cool for 5 minutes before serving.

Avocado Hazelnut Brownies

| Servings: 6 |
| Preparation time: 10 minutes | Cooking time: 18 minutes | Total time: 28 minutes |

Ingredients:

- 1 cup hazelnut flour
- 1 1/2 organic avocado, peeled and cored
- 1/8 teaspoon sea salt
- 4 teaspoons erythritol
- 3/4 teaspoon baking soda
- 1/4 cup cacao powder, raw and unsweetened
- 1/3 chocolate chips, lactose-free
- 1 teaspoon vanilla extract, unsweetened
- 3 tablespoons hazelnut butter
- 1 tablespoon avocado oil

Method:
- Place all the ingredients except for chocolate chips in a food processor and pulse for 1 to 2 minutes at high speed until incorporated.
- Switch on a 6-quarts air fryer, set temperature to 180 degrees C or 350 degrees F and time to 5 minutes to preheat it.
- In the meantime, tip processed brownie mixture into a greased air fryer baking pan, fold in 3/4th of chocolate chips until mixed and then scatter remaining chocolate chips on top.
- Insert baking pan into the air fryer, set frying time to 18 minutes and let cook until top is brown and inserted skewer into the center of brownie come out clean.
- When fryer beeps, remove baking pan from the air fryer and take out brownie.
- Let the brownie cool completely on wire rack, then cut evenly into six pieces and serve.

Lemon Poppy Coffee Cake

| Servings: 1 cake |
| Preparation time: 10 minutes | Cooking time: 15 minutes | Total time: 25 minutes |

Ingredients:

- 1 cups almond flour
- ¼ cup coconut flour
- 2 tablespoons poppy seeds
- ½ teaspoon salt
- ½ cup erythritol sweetener
- ¾ teaspoon baking soda
- 1 teaspoon vanilla extract, unsweetened
- 2 organic lemons, juiced and zested
- 3 eggs, pasture raised
- ¼ cup avocado oil, pure
- ¼ cup coconut milk, unsweetened

Method:
- Place flours in a bowl and stir in salt and baking soda until combined.
- Crack eggs in another bowl and whisk in erythritol, vanilla, lemon juice and zest, oil and coconut milk until combined.
- Gradually stir this mixture into flour mixture until incorporated and then fold in poppy seeds until mixed.
- Switch on a 6-quarts air fryer, set temperature to 180 degrees C or 350 degrees F and time to 5 minutes to preheat it.
- In the meantime, take a Bundt pan, big enough to fit into air fryer basket and grease with oil.
- Spoon cake batter into Bundt pan and place it into air fryer basket.
- Insert fryer basket into the air fryer, set frying time to 15 minutes and let cook until top is nicely brown and inserted skewer into the cake comes out clean.
- When fryer beeps, remove the Bundt pan from air fryer and turn out the cake.
- Let cake cool completely on wire rack before slicing to serve.

Rosemary and Chocolate Bread

| Servings: 1 bread |

| Preparation time: 10 minutes | Cooking time: 30 minutes | Total time: 40 minutes |

Ingredients:

- 2 medium organic avocados, peeled and cored
- 4 organic black mission figs, chopped
- 1/2 cup almond flour
- 1/2 cup coconut flour
- 1 tablespoon arrowroot flour
- 1 tablespoon ground flaxseed meal
- 1/8 teaspoon sea salt
- 1 teaspoon baking powder
- 1 scoop Marine Collagen
- 1/2 cup cacao chocolate chips, raw and lactose-free
- 2 organic rosemary stems, leaves torn
- 1 organic lemon, zested
- 1/2 cup avocado oil, pure
- 2 tablespoons warm water
- 1 egg, pastured raised

Method:

- Stir together flaxseed meal and warm water in a bowl and let rest for five mixtures.
- Place flours in a bowl and stir in salt, baking powder, Marine collagen, chocolate chips and lemon zest until combined.
- Place remaining ingredients in a food processor and pulse for 1 to 2 minutes or until blended.
- Gradually stir this mixture among with flaxseed meal mixture into flour mixture until incorporated and thick dough comes together.
- Switch on a 6-quarts air fryer, set temperature to 180 degrees C or 350 degrees F and time to 5 minutes to preheat it.

- Take a loaf pan big enough to fit into air fryer basket, grease it with oil and spoon in prepared bread batter.
- Place loaf pan into the air fryer basket, then insert it into the air fryer and set frying time to 30 minutes
- Let cook until top is nicely browned and inserted skewer into bread comes out clean.
- When fryer beeps, remove loaf pan from air fryer and take out bread.
- Let bread cool slightly before serving.

Almond Hazelnut Cake with Strawberries

| Servings: 1 cake |
| Preparation time: 15 minutes | Cooking time: 30 minutes | Total time: 45 minutes |

Ingredients:

- 3/4 cup almond flour
- 1/3 cup hazelnuts flour
- 1/4 cup cassava flour
- 2 tablespoons coconut flour
- 4 eggs, pasture raised
- 1 teaspoon baking powder
- 1 teaspoon vanilla extract, unsweetened
- 1/4 cup erythritol
- 1/4 teaspoon sea salt
- 2 tablespoons lemon zest, organic

FOR FILLING

- 1 cup chopped strawberries, organic
- 1/2 cup ground roasted hazelnuts
- 2 tablespoons erythritol
- 1 tablespoons vanilla extract, unsweetened
- 1 cup Italian Mascarpone, lactose-free
- 1 egg, pasture raised
- 1/4 cup organic heavy whipping cream, grass-fed and lactose-free

Method:

- Separate egg yolks and egg whites in two large bowls and beat egg yolks with 2 tablespoons erythritol and ½ teaspoon vanilla until creamy.
- Add remaining erythritol and vanilla to egg whites and beat until stiff peaks form.
- Place flours in another bowl and stir in baking powder, salt, and lemon zest until mixed.
- Stir this mixture into egg yolks, 2 tablespoons at a time, until a hard dough comes together.

- Stir in egg white, 2 tablespoons at a time, until dough turns soft.
- Switch on a 6-quarts air fryer, set temperature to 180 degrees C or 350 degrees F and time to 5 minutes to preheat it.
- In the meantime, grease a cake pan, large enough to fit into air fryer basket and spoon in the prepared cake batter.
- Place cake pan into fryer basket, then insert it into the air fryer and set frying time to 30 minutes.
- Let cook until top is nicely browned and inserted a skewer into bread comes out clean.
- While cake is being cooked, prepare filling.
- For this, separate egg yolks and whites for filling in two separate bowls and beat egg whites until stiff peaks form.
- Add erythritol to egg yolks and beat until creamy.
- Then stir in mascarpone cream, 1 tablespoon at a time, until incorporated and then mix in whipping cream and vanilla.
- Gradually stir in egg white, 2 tablespoons at a time, then put cream in an airtight container and let rest in the refrigerator until required.
- When fryer beeps, remove cake pan from air fryer and take out the cake.
- Let cake slightly and then cut evenly into two layers.
- Spread half of the prepared cream on one top of cake layers, then sprinkle with half of the ground hazelnuts and scatter with half of the strawberries.
- Cover with the second layer, then spread remaining cream on top, scatter with remaining strawberries and sprinkle with hazelnuts.
- Let cake rest in the refrigerator for 4 hours or for a day and then slice to serve.

Ginger Bread Cookies

| Servings: 14 cookies |
| Preparation time: 45 minutes | Cooking time: 24 minutes | Total time: 1 hour & 9 minutes |

Ingredients:

- 2 cups almond flour, blanched
- 3/4 cup coconut flour
- 2 teaspoons ground ginger, organic
- 1/2 teaspoon salt
- 1/2 cup erythritol
- 1 teaspoon allspice, organic
- 1 teaspoon ground cinnamon, organic
- 1/2 teaspoon baking soda
- 1 teaspoon vanilla extract, unsweetened
- 1/2 cup melted coconut oil, cooled
- 2 eggs, pasture raised

FOR ICING
- 1 cup erythritol
- 1/2 teaspoon vanilla extract, unsweetened
- 1 tablespoon almond butter, softened
- 1 tablespoon almond milk, unsweetened

Method:
- Crack eggs in a bowl and whisk in erythritol, vanilla and coconut oil until combined.
- Stir in remaining ingredients for cookies, one at a time, until firm dough comes together and let the dough rest for 30 minutes in the refrigerator.
- Then place a parchment sheet on a clean working space, place dough on it, cover with another parchment sheet and roll dough to ¼-inch thickness using a rolling pin.

- Use medium-sized gingerbread cookie cutter to cut out cookies and place on a baking sheet.
- Roll the remaining dough and cut out more cookies.
- Switch on a 6-quarts air fryer, set temperature to 160 degrees C or 320 degrees F and time to 5 minutes to preheat it.
- Grease air fryer basket with oil, place gingerbread cookies in a single layer and insert fryer basket into the air fryer.
- Set frying time to 8 minutes and let cook until nicely browned.
- When fryer beeps, transfer cookies to wire rack using tongs to cool and cook remaining cookies in the same manner.
- Let cookies cool until turn crunchy.
- In the meantime, whisk together all the ingredients for icing using an electric beater until smooth and then transfer this mixture into piping bag.
- Decorated cooled gingerbread cookies with this icing and serve,

CONCLUSION

Taking a step to improve your health and fitness is not an easy one. If you have decided to go on the lectin-free diet, there will a lot of content on the internet that might discourage you to drop it due to the foods that you will have to eliminate from your diet and the commitment you need to have to stick to this diet is also difficult. Hopefully, this book has helped you demystify the diet and gain true insight about the benefits of this diet.

Made in the USA
Middletown, DE
09 April 2019